MURDER IN THE DARK

MURDER IN
THE DARK

Simon R. Green

This first world edition published 2018
in Great Britain and the USA by
SEVERN HOUSE PUBLISHERS LTD of
Eardley House, 4 Uxbridge Street, London W8 7SY
Trade paperback edition first published
in Great Britain and the USA 2018 by
SEVERN HOUSE PUBLISHERS LTD

British Library Cataloguing in Publication Data
A CIP catalogue record for this title is available from the British Library.

ISBN-13: 978-0-7278-8823-5 (cased)
ISBN-13: 978-1-84751-948-1 (trade paper)
ISBN-13: 978-1-4483-0158-4 (e-book)

This is a work of fiction. Names, characters, places and incidents
are either the product of the author's imagination or are used fictitiously.
Except where actual historical events and characters are being described
for the storyline of this novel, all situations in this publication are
fictitious and any resemblance to actual persons, living or dead,
business establishments, events or locales is purely coincidental.

All Severn House titles are printed on acid-free paper.

Severn House Publishers support the Forest Stewardship Council™ [FSC™],
the leading international forest certification organisation.
All our titles that are printed on FSC certified paper carry the FSC logo.

MIX
Paper from
responsible sources
FSC
www.fsc.org   FSC® C013056

Typeset by Palimpsest Book Production Ltd.,
Falkirk, Stirlingshire, Scotland.
Printed and bound in Great Britain by
TJ International, Padstow, Cornwall.

Prologue

Call me Ishmael. Ishmael Jones.
In 1963 an alien ship crashed to Earth, and the sole survivor was made human by transformation machines. I have walked this world ever since, remembering nothing of my previous existence. To help me hide from today's surveillance-heavy society, I work for the mysterious Organization, investigating cases of the weird and unusual.

There are all kinds of stories concerning people who disappear mysteriously, never to be seen again. Sometimes the accusing finger points to fairy rings or bad places; others prefer to lay the blame on mythical beings or alien abductions. Strange out of the way locations where people encounter terrible holes in the structure of the world are the only thing these stories have in common. Are these mysterious holes traps for the unwary, or doors to other realities? Either way, who or what is waiting on the other side?

Some parts of the world are older than others. The south-west of England is so old it qualifies as ancient, which is probably why its history is so heavily packed with monsters and mysteries. Back in the sixth century, it was the last Celtic territory to fall to the invading Saxons. Before that, the Romans built roads, aqueducts and cities, trying to hold back the unknown with the solid sanity of civilization. Go back even further and you can find great circles of standing stones like Avebury and Stonehenge, and Neolithic burial sites where they weighed down their dead with heavy rocks to keep them from walking.

The past is England's dreaming, and not all of it sleeps soundly. There are all kinds of things left over from when the world was a different place. In my time as a field agent for the Organization I've dealt with any number of strange and *unnatural threats, walking steadfastly into trouble and danger to put down the kind of things no one else can. History isn't always over. Not when it can wait with remorseless patience for one more chance to get its claws into you.*

ONE
The Hole in the Hill

I hate being sent out on missions without a proper briefing. But when the Colonel calls me in the early hours of the morning using the phone number no one else even knows exists and says 'Go now!', then I get up and go. Because that's part of the agreement I entered into when the Organization first agreed to take me under its wing: that they would send me into harm's way on a regular basis and I would never say no, because it was always going to be something that needed doing.

Which was how, on a pleasant summer's afternoon, I came to be speeding through the wilds of Somerset with my partner, Penny Belcourt. People like me aren't supposed to have partners, for any number of really good reasons; but since there are no people like me, I feel free to make the rules up as I go along.

Penny was at the wheel, because no one is allowed to drive any of her precious vintage cars but her. So I just settled down in the passenger seat and enjoyed the ride and the countryside. The pastel-blue sky was slowly losing its colour as the afternoon darkened into evening, but the fields on either side of the narrow road were almost luminously green. Grass that really enjoyed being grass. Here and there sheep clustered together for company, and the occasional rabbit stuck its head up for a good look round. No people, no farm machinery, nothing to disturb the pleasant languor of a country afternoon.

And so many trees, everywhere I looked. Tall and heavy, with wide-spreading branches weighed down with summer leaves. People forget that most of England used to be one big primordial forest; until their ancestors cut most of it down because it got in the way. I like trees. When you've been around as long as I have and seen so many things and people disappear, you like to think there are some things that might outlast you.

There was a time when I preferred cities to the countryside. In my early days it was a lot easier to hide in the hustle and bustle of a city as just another face in the crowd; whereas a man on his own, a stranger, would always stand out in the small towns and villages. But these days, the ever present surveillance cameras lining the city streets make it a lot harder to pass unnoticed. I'm actually better off in the countryside, where I only have to worry about people seeing me, not cameras.

I glanced across at Penny. She was scowling at the winding road ahead, clearly still not at all happy about being sent out on a case without at least some idea of what we were getting ourselves into. When I turned up at her London flat at what was still far too early in the morning for civilized people, rousted her out of bed, stuck a mug of black coffee in her hand and told her we were needed, her first reaction was that the Colonel was taking advantage of me.

It's true, he does; but to be fair, I take advantage of him, too. It's that kind of relationship.

'Why didn't the Colonel show up in person to brief you?' said Penny. 'He never misses a chance to lecture you about things you don't know, so he can lord it over you.'

'Not always,' I said. 'Not when it's really urgent.'

'It can't be that important,' said Penny. 'At least, no one's died yet. So we can be sure it's not a murder mystery, for once.'

'That's what you said last time,' I said.

She took her eyes off the road for a dangerously long moment, to give me what could only be described as a threateningly cool glare. 'I thought we'd agreed none of that was my fault.'

'Of course,' I said. 'Not your fault in any way, shape or form. Could have happened to anyone.'

She smiled, and turned her attention back to the road. 'You know, you learn faster than a lot of my old boyfriends.'

I thought about that. It seemed there were certain implications there . . . But in the end I just nodded. It seemed safest.

'So,' said Penny. 'All you got this time was a phone call out of the blue and the bare essentials?'

'Apparently we'll be told all we need to know when we get there,' I said. 'So feel free to take your foot off the accelerator now and again. I would prefer to arrive with all my various pieces still attached to each other.'

'You're the one who made such a fuss about the mission being terribly pressing.' Penny slowed the car by a few miles an hour, to show willing. 'It's just . . . there's something about this whole situation that grates on my nerves. Like my subconscious is waving a really big warning flag. It's not like the Colonel to drop you in the deep end without at least some idea of where the sharks are.'

'No,' I said. 'It isn't. Except when it's urgent.'

I smiled across at Penny. I always like looking at her. A striking young woman with a pretty face, strong bone structure, and a mass of night-black hair piled up on top of her head. Dark flashing eyes and a dazzling smile, a trim figure, a stylish look, and enough nervous energy to intimidate anyone who can't keep up with her. She was currently wearing a smart navy-blue business suit, and looked almost frighteningly professional and efficient. Because I'd told her we would be working with scientists; and she was determined not to appear out of her depth. I was wearing my usual dark blazer and slacks, for much the same reason. And because I've never understood the fashion thing.

Penny and I walk side by side into the most dangerous parts of the world on a regular basis, and it's a matter of pride to both of us that we never blink first. We uncover secrets, solve mysteries, and do our best to protect people from things that shouldn't exist but unfortunately do. I see things from the outside, and she understands the complexities of the human heart. We work well together; because nothing can hide from both of us.

I looked at myself in the rear-view mirror. I always feel a faint hint of surprise when I see my reflection, as though what I'm seeing isn't what I expected. Tall, dark, and handsome enough if you're not too choosy; a pleasantly anonymous look that allows me to move through the world without being noticed. Because I can't afford to be noticed. I can't have people asking questions, because I don't have any answers. I've spent most of my life investigating mysteries, but I've never even come close to understanding the most important one of all: who or, perhaps more properly, what I really am. Perhaps because when you get right down to it, I don't want to know.

'I think I've been patient long enough,' said Penny. 'It's time to tell me what you do know. What are we doing way out here, miles from anywhere?'

'We're to provide security for an archaeological dig on Brassknocker Hill, just outside the city of Bath,' I said. 'It seems this particular team of shovellers and trowel experts were busy digging up some farmer's field in search of an old Roman villa when they stumbled across something far more interesting. A hole in the side of the hill with unnatural properties.'

'How can a hole be unnatural?' said Penny.

'That's the point, isn't it?' I said cheerfully. 'If it was just an ordinary hole in the ground, the Organization wouldn't be sending us in. The only other piece of information I possess is that one of the archaeologists fell into this hole and apparently disappeared.'

'As in missing, presumed dead?' said Penny.

'Apparently,' I said. 'Not a trace of him to be found anywhere.'

'So we're talking about a really deep hole,' said Penny. 'Some kind of cave-in, perhaps?'

'Perhaps,' I said, just to be polite. 'I think the key word here is "unnatural". It's not a word the Organization tends to use lightly. Perhaps the hole ate him.'

'Oh, ick!' said Penny.

'The surviving archaeologists have been removed from the site and replaced with a Government-sponsored scientific team.'

'Hold it! The Organization can call on official scientific teams for help?' said Penny. 'How long has that been going on?'

'Beats the hell out of me,' I said. 'The Colonel only tells me what he thinks I need to know, and I don't always believe all of that. The Organization seems determined to remain the greatest mystery of all.'

'Even to those who work for it?' said Penny.

I had to smile. 'Perhaps especially to those who work for it.'

Penny sniffed loudly, and put the car through an expert but unnecessary racing gear change as she swept round a tight corner. The Romans might have liked their roads straight, but country roads have always favoured the winding way and the sharp unexpected turn. Preferably with something unnerving on the other side. Penny shot me a quick look.

'Not for the first time, it occurs to me that you should have asked a lot more questions before you agreed to join the Organization.'

'It wasn't like I had much of a choice,' I said. 'They found me when I thought no one could. And I'd run out of secret groups willing and able to run the necessary interference between me and the security systems that watch the world every minute of every day. For your own good, of course. It's become a lot harder for people like me to stay under the radar.'

'There are no people like you . . .' said Penny, automatically. 'Anyway, what do you know about these scientists looking into the hole?'

'They're lead by a Professor Sharon Bellman.'

'Professor of what, exactly? Archaeology, history, sudden strange holes that eat people?'

'Almost certainly one of those,' I said. 'We'll just have to ask when we meet her. She's supposed to fill us in on exactly what's been happening. Hopefully including what's so damned urgent about a hole.'

'What happened to the archaeologists who got replaced?' said Penny.

'The Colonel didn't say, but they've probably been bribed with Government funding and pressured into keeping quiet.'

'If this hole is so dangerous,' said Penny, 'why don't they just hire a concrete mixer and fill it in?'

'No doubt Professor Bellman will tell us,' I said. 'But if the solution was that simple, they wouldn't need us, would they?'

'It still doesn't sound like a murder mystery,' said Penny. 'We already know who did it. The hole.'

'But we don't know how or why,' I said. 'Or whether there could be someone behind this poor unfortunate's disappearance into a hungry hole.'

'He probably just tripped and fell in,' said Penny. 'What do you want to bet that drinking was involved?'

'Are we nearly there yet?'

'Don't start.' She glanced at the satnav, which was sulking in silence on the dashboard because where we were heading wasn't on any official map. 'We just passed Claverton, so we need to start looking for a sharp right turn into Brassknocker Hill.' She broke off, frowning. 'I'm sure I know that name from somewhere.'

'There have been a number of intriguing stories about the Beast of Brassknocker,' I said.

'Yes!' said Penny. 'I remember! I saw a documentary about it on BBC Two. Some vicious and almost certainly apocryphal creature roams the area, eating the livestock and putting the wind up the locals.'

'There's rather more to it than that,' I said. 'There have been any number of sightings and encounters, going back centuries. Disturbing tales of something large and powerful that tears apart the local wildlife, leaving the body parts scattered across the fields. It's also been known to carry off the occasional traveller careless enough to be caught out after dark. Sometimes a hat or a shoe is left behind, but never even a drop of blood. Vicious claw marks have been found, gouged into the doors of farmers' cottages overnight, where something has tried to get in.

'The Beast comes and goes. Sometimes it's not seen for centuries, but it always come back. A thing of silent horror, that haunts the night on Brassknocker Hill for reasons of its own. The last modern sighting was in 1979.'

'What is this Beast supposed to look like?' said Penny.

'Nobody knows,' I said. 'The few reported sightings are pretty basic. Big and strong, all teeth and claws. The usual.'

'How could something like that move around unnoticed?'

'A normal beast couldn't,' I said. 'Which suggests its

origins are probably otherworldly. Unless it's all just a legend.'

Penny shot me a thoughtful look. 'And you just happen to have all this information on the tip of your tongue.'

'I had time to do a little research before we left,' I said. 'I love internet cafés.'

'You think the Beast might be connected with this unnatural hole?'

'I don't know. It's possible.'

'Did you bring a gun?' said Penny. 'I could use a new rug for my front room.'

'I'm an investigator of the unknown, not a big-game hunter.'

'You've never been fond of guns, have you?' said Penny.

'I can use one if I have to,' I said. 'I just prefer not to, mostly.'

'Because you identify with the hunted, and not the hunter?'

'Perhaps,' I said. 'But whether we find ourselves facing a legendary Beast, a human killer, or just a hole with an appetite . . . Let's try to save at least one of the people involved, this time.'

'You're not still brooding over our last case, are you?' said Penny. 'It wasn't your fault everybody died. It was a very tricky case. What matters is you solved the mystery and caught the killers.'

'But not in time to save anyone,' I said. 'I'm getting really tired of watching good people die on my watch because I couldn't solve the mystery fast enough.'

'It's in the nature of the cases they give us,' Penny said carefully. 'They're always going to be the difficult ones. And it's a tribute to you that they know they can rely on you to get to the truth of what's happening.'

'But not always in time to save everyone who needs saving.'

'You can only do what you can do,' Penny said firmly.

'I can try harder,' I said.

'You always do, darling.'

We drove on. It was getting late, and the warmth was going out of the day. Heavy trees lined the road on both sides now. It was like driving through a shadowy green tunnel, and some-times the longer branches would dip down and trail along the roof and sides of the car, as if checking out what we were. The sky became a much darker blue, with heavy cloud moving slowly but remorselessly in from the east. The turning on to Brassknocker Hill was signposted well in advance, but Penny still waited till the very last moment to send the car screeching round the sharp corner. She slammed down through the gears, put her foot down hard, and the engine roared as we hammered up a steep incline. At least one in three. Penny grinned broadly as she threw the car into the first of many bends, not giving a damn whether there might be anything coming the other way. I sighed resignedly as I was pressed back into my seat by the acceleration.

'It feels like we're taking off for Mars,' I said.

'You should know, space boy,' said Penny. 'Now guess whether I give a damn. I'm spy girl, off on another secret mission, and I can't wait to get stuck in!'

The car's engine complained loudly as it struggled with the steep climb. The whole chassis shook with the strain; or possibly with outrage at how it was being treated. I was starting to wonder if the car would hold together long enough to get us where we were going. For reasons best known to herself, Penny had chosen to drive one of the more modern models in her collection; a navy-blue Rover 25. Basically just a box on wheels, conspicuously lacking in style, charm or character. But it didn't half go when Penny put her foot down. Possibly because it was afraid not to.

'What is this fascination of yours for more . . . mature vehicles?' I said. If only to take my mind off the prospect of sudden death in an unanticipated collision, and quite possibly a raging fireball.

'Older cars don't have computers,' said Penny. 'Every time a friend of mine tells me their vehicle is in for repairs, it's never anything mechanical. It's always the computers. Time was if you had a breakdown you just called the AA, and a nice man in uniform would turn up and fix the problem right there at the side of the road. These days, all they can do is shake their heads and tow you to the nearest garage. *Oh, you little shit!*'

She slammed on the brakes. I was thrown forward against

my seat belt, and then slammed back in my seat again. We'd just caught up with a much slower-moving car straining to get up the hill. In the wrong gear, from the sound of it. Penny said something very rude, involving a taboo sexual practice that isn't nearly as much fun as it sounds, and glared venomously at the car in front.

'I hate cars that do thirty miles an hour in a forty limit! And always when there isn't enough room to overtake!'

'You've got that ramming-speed look in your eyes again,' I said carefully. 'Do I really need to remind you that spy girls are not supposed to do anything that might get them noticed?'

'And as for people who only do thirty in a fifty zone – *It's clearly marked, you unspeakable moron!* – you should be legally entitled to drive them off the road, drag the driver out of the wreckage, and then beat them about the head with a tyre iron until their brains start working. In fact, you should be legally obliged to do it, to help clear out the murkier depths of the gene pool.'

'Breathe, Penny, breathe,' I said kindly.

Clearly picking up on the mood of the driver behind him, the car ahead found a different gear and speeded up. Penny stuck close behind it, just to make sure it didn't suffer a relapse, and we roared up the long winding road together as though the Beast itself was in hot pursuit. Penny was so intent on the driver in front she missed the sign we'd been told to look for, and I had to point it out to her. She stamped on the brakes again, spun the wheel round, and sent the Rover hurtling through the open wooden gate without slowing. The car bumped and skidded across a grassy slope, the rear wheels throwing up heavy divots of earth as the brakes kicked in, until we finally slammed to a halt.

'Next time, I'll drive,' I said.

'Over my dead body.'

'That's what's worrying me.'

'We're here, aren't we?' Penny peered through the windscreen. 'There doesn't seem to be a designated parking area. Or any other vehicles.'

'Let's just leave the car here,' I said. 'Give it a chance to get its breath back. We can walk the rest of the way.'

Penny shut down the engine with something of a flourish, and a blessed quiet prevailed. The car's chassis made loud ticking noises as it settled, as if in protest at such brutal treatment, but Penny ignored it. She expected her cars to be able to look after themselves. We got out of the Rover and looked around. The long grassy slope of Brassknocker Hill stretched endlessly down to a valley below, entirely untouched by civilization or even grazing animals, and finally a series of open fields and a deserted railway line. It all seemed very peaceful. Penny moved in close beside me and slipped an arm through mine as we enjoyed the scenery.

I've always liked the countryside. It's big enough for anyone to get lost in.

'You'd better lock the car,' I said.

Penny already had the key fob in her hand, but now she looked at me suspiciously.

'Why? We're halfway up a hill in the middle of nowhere.'

'Just in case,' I said.

'You think the Beast is going to get in and drive it away?'

'I've seen stranger things,' I said. 'And so have you.'

Penny hit the remote on the fob, and all the locks slammed down.

Then we both looked round sharply, as a loud and hearty voice called out to us. A short, sturdy middle-aged woman was striding down the hill, waving a hand to catch our attention, as though there was a chance we might miss the only moving thing on the landscape. By the time she reached us, she was moving so quickly that she had to dig both heels in hard to stop herself, and then she smiled at both of us in a somewhat overbearing way. She had a broad, determined face under a crop of greying blonde hair, and was wearing a sensible tweed suit and muddy wellington boots. She had the look of a woman who got things done, whether other people liked it or not. She insisted on shaking both of us by the hand, with a frankly masculine handshake.

'Hello, hello!' she said vigorously, looking back and forth between us as though trying to decide which of us most needed impressing. 'Ishmael Jones and Penny Belcourt? Correct? Thought so! I'm Professor Bellman. I've been put in charge of this mess, for my sins. Call me Professor, it helps keep the others in line. No problem getting here? Good, good . . . So, you're the Organization people?'

Which was not a question I was used to getting from apparent civilians.

'Who told you that?' I said.

'The Colonel, of course,' said the Professor.

I felt I had to raise an eyebrow. 'You know the Colonel? Not many do.'

'Just as well,' said the Professor. 'Of course, I don't know the current fellow. He was just a voice on the phone in the middle of the night. All my dealings were with the previous chap. I did some research for the Organization, back in the day.'

'What kind of research?' said Penny.

'The kind I'm still not allowed to talk about,' said the Professor.

'That's the Organization for you,' I said.

'I thought they'd forgotten all about me,' said the Professor. 'But apparently once an asset, always an asset.'

'Not necessarily,' I said.

There must have been something in my voice, because Penny quickly decided to cut in.

'Why did the Colonel want you for this job, Professor?'

'I made my reputation doing theoretical work on dimensional doorways,' said the Professor. 'Cutting-edge stuff at the time. But, of course, that was years and years ago.'

I looked at her thoughtfully. The situation had just taken a turn I hadn't expected.

'And that's what you think we have here?'

'Could be, could be,' said the Professor. 'I'm glad you've finally turned up. We could use a fresh pair of eyes, and some new ideas. We've been working at this for . . . Damn me . . . fourteen hours straight, with absolutely nothing useful to show for it. Come with me and I'll introduce you to the team. They're all dying to meet you.'

She turned abruptly and strode away, back up the hill. She leaned right over into the incline, grunting with the effort, and didn't look back once to make sure we were following. So I stayed put, and looked at Penny.

'Is it just me, or did she not sound entirely convincing about her team wanting to meet us?'

'It's not just you,' said Penny. 'And . . . the hole is now a door between dimensions? That's a whole other step up from a possible cave-in that someone might have fallen into.'

'Maybe it's nothing to do with the Beast, after all,' I said. 'Though I suppose it could involve a white rabbit . . .'

'Don't even go there!' said Penny.

We moved off after the Professor, deliberately not hurrying. Never jump to obey when people start barking orders, they'll only take advantage. The Professor had already disappeared over a sharp rise in the ground, and when Penny and I climbed over it we found her waiting for us beside the original archaeological dig. Some distance further up the hill, five young people were working at a variety of scientific equipment, arranged and racked together under a very basic structure that did little more than provide a flat roof, four clear-plastic walls, and some protection from the elements. None of the scientists even glanced up from what they were doing, though they must have heard us approaching. The Professor waited impatiently for us to join her, then lowered her voice to what she apparently considered a confidential level. But she had the kind of voice that travelled, and her team would have had to be deaf as well as really dumb not to have heard every word.

'They're all good people,' she said. 'First-class minds. Though it would probably have helped if they'd been volunteers, instead of being pressed.'

I nodded understandingly. 'The Colonel twisted some arms to get you and your people here?'

'He put the fear of God into me,' said the Professor. 'I told him I was far too old for fieldwork, and he told me he didn't care. Either I got my arse in gear or he would tell the University about a few things I might have done back when I was a student and a little too political. I really do feel there should be a statute of limitations on how long you can be expected to pay for the crimes of your youth. I wasn't even that bad, just . . . enthusiastic.' She sniffed loudly. 'He even had a car bring me straight here, to make sure I wouldn't get lost along the way.'

'Your team doesn't look old enough to have that many sins of youth to worry about,' I said.

The Professor scowled. 'You're never too young to make mistakes you'd rather the world never finds out about. Especially in the academic world. And before you ask . . . No, I don't know why any of them agreed to join our merry band. Don't ask, don't tell. Isn't that what they say?'

I realized Penny was looking at me.

'Has the Colonel ever pressured you into doing something you didn't want to do, Ishmael?' she asked carefully.

'That was never part of our agreement,' I said. 'And besides, he wouldn't dare. I'd punch him through a wall if he crossed the line, and he knows it.'

'So,' said the Professor, in her open and hearty way that might or might not have been genuine. 'Do you have any idea why it's so damned necessary we come up with answers to this particular mystery?'

'No,' I said. 'Though I will say, the Colonel isn't one to panic easily. If he thinks this is important, it probably is.'

'Tell us about this unusual hole,' Penny said to the Professor. 'Does it really eat people?'

The Professor looked at her coolly. 'As far as I know, the missing archaeologist simply got a little too close and fell in. But we're still treating the hole with the greatest of respect, and even more caution. And when you've seen it, you'll understand why. In fact, I think you need to see it before you meet the team. It'll help you put all of this in the proper context.'

She set off up the hill again, carefully choosing a path that would give her people a wide berth, and we followed after her. The young scientists remained determinedly intent on their work.

'The Colonel said there was something unnatural about the hole,' I said.

'Good word,' said the Professor. 'Another good word would be pants-wettingly disturbing.'

'How deep does it go?' said Penny.

'No idea,' said the Professor. 'Just one of the many things we don't know about it, including how it's able to defy so

many laws of physics simultaneously without even
apologizing.'

'What kind of hole are we talking about?' I said.

'I'm not even convinced it is a hole,' said the Professor.
And then she increased her pace, so she wouldn't have to
answer any more questions.

We made our way through the original archaeological dig.
Disturbed earth, shallow trenches, and marked-off areas showing
sections of revealed stone wall. Plus a glimpse of what might
have been a floor mosaic. The Professor barely glanced at any
of it.

'An important and significant historical find, or so I'm told.
Not my line of expertise. Try not to trip over any of it.'

'It looks like they left in a hurry,' said Penny.

'Wouldn't you if you'd just lost one of your own to an
unexplained phenomenon?' said the Professor. 'Besides, I don't
suppose the Organization gave them much choice in the matter.
For their own good, of course.'

'Of course,' I said.

The Professor shot a quick look at her people, as we drew
nearer.

'The equipment's a bit basic. It was all set up and waiting
for us when we got here. I've been assured better stuff is
on the way, but my feeling is they didn't want to risk anything
too expensive this close to the hole. It's expendable, just
like us.'

'Speak for yourself,' I said.

'Hear! Hear!' said Penny. 'Just how dangerous is this hole,
which we are currently moving towards perhaps a little more
quickly than necessary?'

'You'll be safe enough,' said the Professor. 'As long as you
keep your distance. And your guard up.'

'And don't fall in,' I said.

'Exactly!' said the Professor.

We passed half a dozen small tents, huddled together on
the side of the hill as though for comfort.

'They're a bit rough and ready,' said the Professor. 'I thought
we'd be booked into some nice little hotel at a nearby town,
but no . . . I can only suppose someone decided keeping us

isolated here would prevent us from getting too loose-lipped with the locals.'

'What kind of equipment are you using to study the hole?' asked Penny.

'Oh, sensory devices,' said the Professor. 'For measuring all kinds of things.'

Penny glared at her coldly. 'Could you be any more condescending?'

'If you like,' said the Professor.

I stopped as we finally drew level with the scientists in their improvised equipment centre, and Penny stopped with me. The Professor kept going, hoping to carry us along with her, but when Penny and I made it clear we weren't budging she had no choice but to stop as well. I studied the scientists carefully. Four men, one woman. So young the ink was probably still wet on their diplomas. I couldn't help noticing they were all sticking to their own particular pieces of equipment, as though guarding their territory. Concentrating on their own work, and showing no interest in sharing their findings. Ambitious and driven. A dangerous combination.

They were all wearing heavy anoraks. I looked at Penny.

'I told you to wear something heavier, because it was bound to be cold out in the open.'

'Oh, shut up!' said Penny. 'Just because you don't feel the cold. Why have we stopped?'

'Because the Professor is right. They should have better equipment to work with than that.'

'You really think the Organization sees this hole as so dangerous that they're prepared to write us all off as expendable?'

'That's always a possibility in our line of work, but I'm getting a really bad feeling about this one . . .'

'We could always walk away,' Penny said quietly. 'Hell! We could run back to the car and then drive away at great speed. Or do you think someone would turn up to stop us?'

'Let's take a look at the hole first,' I said. 'See if it's worth all this paranoia.'

'If you've quite finished gawping at my little group of *enfants terribles*, the hole is waiting,' said the Professor.

'I thought they were looking forward to meeting us?' Penny said innocently. 'So far, they haven't even waved.'

'They're very busy,' said the Professor. 'We're all operating under a lot of pressure. I will introduce you properly, once you've taken a look at the hole. Because then you'll understand just how much trouble we're in.'

She started moving again, but I didn't. I'd just spotted a massive steel drum standing on its own, half-hidden behind the tents, with a hell of a lot of steel cable wound around it. An engine had been attached to one side, so the cable could be unwound at a controlled rate and then pulled back again. The drum had been secured to the hillside by a number of heavy steel bolts driven into the ground. The whole thing looked very out of place, even ominous, in such a pastoral setting. I turned to the Professor for an explanation, and she shrugged briefly.

'We've been lowering things into the hole. Various pieces of equipment, and a number of test animals.'

I tried to estimate how much cable was wrapped around the drum, and didn't like the answer I was getting. 'Just how deep is this hole?'

'We don't know,' said the Professor. She sounded suddenly tired, even depressed. 'We try to go a little deeper every time, and have found that each time we can go deeper. I'm tempted to say we might be out of our depth here.'

Penny pointed silently but meaningfully at a collection of animal cages stacked beside the drum. They were all empty. The Professor shrugged briefly. I was starting to think that was her standard response to most questions.

'We used them all up,' she said. 'None left.'

'What happened to them?' said Penny, in a voice that suggested she already knew the answer and wasn't at all happy about it.

'No idea,' said the Professor. 'We've sent for some more. They should be here tomorrow.'

'What kind of animals have you been using?' said Penny.

'Guinea pigs, mice, birds, even a few of the larger insects,' said the Professor. 'No cats or dogs. Nothing cute enough for anyone to give a damn. Can we please get a move on?'

We followed her up the hill. And there, finally, was the hole. Nothing too impressive, at first glance. Just a large dark circle in the sloping grass. The Professor stopped a good four feet short of the hole, and insisted we did the same. She pointed to a line at our feet that had been gouged deeply into the earth.

'This is as far as we go. It's not safe to get any closer.'

I studied the hole carefully. Set neatly into the side of the hill, like a small cave, it had to be at least seven feet in diameter. But it took me only a moment to decide there was nothing natural about it. The perimeter was a perfect circle, as if it had been cut out of the grassy slope with some kind of machine. But there was no sign of debris, and no crumbling earth at the edges.

The darkness that filled the hole was unnervingly complete. The daylight didn't penetrate one inch. It was like looking at a night sky with no moon and no stars. Just a darkness that went on for ever. I didn't need to be told this hole was dangerous. The dark in the hole wasn't merely the absence of light; it was a thing in its own right. It looked . . . wrong. It didn't belong in the everyday world where things were supposed to make sense.

'It's like looking into a bottomless pit,' Penny said quietly. 'Except . . . Ishmael, do you get the feeling it's looking back at us?'

'Everyone feels that,' said the Professor. 'Like the hole is studying us while we're studying it. The only thing my team and I can agree on is that this is a hole in the world, not just the hill. Come over here.'

She led us off to one side, still careful to maintain a respectful distance. Someone had dug a ragged hole in the ground, a couple of feet in diameter, with perfectly normal crumbling edges. A reassuringly human effort. I studied it carefully.

'That's not just a hole. It's a tunnel through the earth.'

'You've got good eyes,' said the Professor. 'Yes, it's a tunnel. Goes right through the hill, behind the hole, and emerges on the other side. Demonstrating that although the hole itself goes down a disturbingly long way, it isn't descending into the earth. It's going somewhere else. Some of my people think it's an opening into another world.'

'Is that what you think?' I said.

'Perhaps,' said the Professor. 'Perhaps.'

I got down on one knee, and thrust my right arm as far into the tunnel as it would go. I jerked my hand back and forth, banging it against the earth sides of the tunnel while looking at the hole above it, but the hole remained entirely unmoved by what I was doing. Penny looked apologetically at the Professor.

'Sorry. Ishmael always has to check everything for himself.'

'Don't worry,' said the Professor. 'We all had a try. Just to convince ourselves the hole wasn't some kind of optical illusion.'

'It isn't,' I said, pulling my arm out of the tunnel and getting to my feet again. 'Wherever this hole goes, it's not anywhere in our world.'

The Professor marched us back in front of the hole, careful to keep us behind the safety line, and we all stood and stared at the flat impenetrable darkness.

'And this is what the missing archaeologist disappeared into?' I said finally.

'Went in and never came out,' said the Professor.

'Did anyone try going in after him?' said Penny.

'Would you?' said the Professor. 'You only have to look at that thing to know it's not safe.'

'Then why did the archaeologist get so close?' I said.

'Good question,' said the Professor.

'Did they try shouting after him?' said Penny.

'According to the official report, they shouted themselves hoarse,' said the Professor. 'But there was no response from inside the hole. Not then, or since. We've been listening to it on every frequency there is, without any result.'

'Has anything emerged from the hole?' I said.

'No,' said the Professor.

'Has the size of the hole ever changed?' said Penny.

'Good question,' said the Professor. 'No. Nothing about the hole has changed since it first appeared. And before you ask, none of the archaeologists saw it appear. They just turned round and there it was. Looking like it had always been there.'

We stood before the hole for a while, studying it in silence.

There was something blunt and obtrusive about this thing that had forced its way into our world. As though it didn't care, because there was nothing we could do to stop it doing whatever it was there to do.

'My team has been tasked to discover what the hole is, what it's for and, most important of all, what might be on the other side,' the Professor said finally. 'We are all very determined and extremely motivated to get to the bottom of this hole. It's been made very clear to us that our future careers depend on coming up with some answers.'

'Your original work on dimensional doorways . . .' I said. 'Was it entirely theoretical?'

'Of course!' she said. 'I never thought to see one in the flesh, so to speak. I was just trying to work out what kind of circumstances might produce or support such phenomena. Have you ever seen anything like this before?'

'No,' I said. 'But I think I understand why the Colonel was in such a rush. This could be a weak spot in the physical state of the universe, where two worlds touch. It could even be an entrance point for an invasion from somewhere else. Or, to take a more positive view, it could help us understand how to travel to such other places. Very valuable information; or very dangerous, in the wrong hands. No wonder the Colonel wanted some security in place as soon as possible.'

'Let's not get ahead of ourselves,' said the Professor. 'This could be an entirely natural phenomenon. The maths allows for it, though that's just another area of science we don't properly understand yet. We haven't found any positive proof of aliens.'

'Is there anything you are certain of?' said Penny.

'Yes. The hole's edges are razor-sharp.'

The Professor bent down and picked up a long branch that had been left lying on the ground, just inside the safety line. She straightened up, took one careful step across the line, then jabbed the branch at the right-hand edge of the hole. The end was immediately cut through, and the severed part disappeared into the hole. There was no sense of transition as the end of the branch entered the darkness; it was just suddenly gone. The Professor stepped quickly back behind the line again.

'Now that's interesting,' I said. 'There was no sense of resistance, the end sheared through immediately. And the severed part dropped into the hole, not to the ground.'

'Well spotted,' said the Professor, letting the branch fall to the ground. 'We've tried this several times, and the end always goes in. It seems there's some kind of pull or gravity involved. Another good reason for the safety line.'

'What about the archaeologist?' said Penny. 'Could the hole's gravity have pulled him in?'

'Nobody saw it happen,' said the Professor.

She glared at the hole, as though accusing it of keeping secrets from her just to be annoying. Penny leaned in close to me.

'Can you see anything inside the hole, Ishmael? Are you picking up anything from it?'

'I can't see one inch past the surface,' I said quietly. 'And I'm not hearing anything, either. I'm not sure the hole is actually *there*, as we understand the word. I think what we're seeing might only be our minds attempting to interpret something entirely outside our experience.'

'As answers go, that really didn't help,' said Penny.

'I know,' I said. 'Professor! Could the appearance of the hole be linked to what the archaeologists were digging up at the time?'

'That was one of the first things the Colonel asked me to look into,' said the Professor. 'There's no obvious connection. And nothing in the ground they disturbed seems in any way out of the ordinary.'

'What was a Roman villa doing all the way out here?' I said. 'We're a long way from the main Roman settlement in Bath.'

I looked back down the hill to the archaeological dig.

'Why did the Romans feel the need to build a villa halfway up a hill miles from anywhere? To watch something? Or watch out for something that might appear? Was there a hole, and perhaps even a Beast, all those centuries ago?'

'And how did the archaeologists know to dig here in the first place?' said Penny.

'More good questions,' said the Professor. 'Though I only

have an answer to the last one. A local farmer was searching
for buried treasure with a metal detector. He found some old
Roman coins here, had them checked by someone at the
University of Bath, and they supplied the archaeological team.'

'How close is this man's farm?' I said.

'Over three miles away,' said the Professor. 'He's been
warned to keep his distance till this is all over. He doesn't
know about the hole.' And then she paused, choosing her
words carefully. 'There are quite a few local legends about
mysterious disappearances, going back centuries. Perhaps this
hole has been here before. We could be looking at a recurring
phenomenon, a hole that moves in time rather than space,
reappearing at this particular location on a regular basis. Do
you have anything to add?'

'Not for the moment,' I said. Glad of a chance to get a word
in edgeways.

The Professor fixed me with a hard look. 'If you've been
sent to whip us on to greater efforts, you're wasting your time,'
she said flatly. 'My people are already working flat out.'

'We're here to protect you, not pressure you,' I said.

The Professor looked down the hill at her scientists, still
entirely absorbed in their work. 'They're good kids. Doing
their best under impossible conditions. All our scans of the
hole have proved useless, and any instruments we lower into
the hole don't work. It's possible that once you get inside, the
very laws of physics are different . . .' She turned back, to
present me with a less confrontational gaze. 'Is there any
chance you could talk to the Colonel? We need better equipment and more of it to do our work properly. And we need it
now, not tomorrow.'

'I'm sorry,' I said. 'The Colonel and I don't have that kind
of relationship. I just go where I'm told, and do what I'm told.
Mostly. Has he given you a deadline?'

'If my original theories are correct, the hole will only remain
here for a maximum of forty hours,' the Professor said carefully. 'And twenty-two of those hours have already passed.'

'No wonder the Colonel was in such a hurry,' I said.

'What happens if you can't produce any answers in time?'
said Penny.

'We won't be allowed back when the hole reappears,' said the Professor. 'Some other group of bright young minds will get their chance. That's the real reason we're all working so hard. This is the kind of work that makes careers, not to mention reputations. What we learn here could rewrite the physics books. Come and meet the team. Let them tell you what they've been doing.'

'You go on,' I said. 'We'll join you in a while.'

The Professor shrugged briefly, and set off down the hillside to the equipment centre. I studied the hole carefully. Penny stood close beside me, her arm tucked through mine, as if to ground herself in the face of something so distinctly otherworldly. The darkness of the hole turned my gaze aside effortlessly, a flat black surface that seemed almost two-dimensional. But there was no denying the hole had a definite presence: just by being there it had an impact on the world. I found it difficult to tear my eyes away. Because while it was there, nothing else was as important.

I deliberately turned my gaze away, and looked at Penny.

'What do you see when you look at the hole?' I said carefully.

'A stain on the world,' she said immediately. 'Something that shouldn't be here. Unnatural, just like the Colonel said. What do you see?'

'Something alien.'

'Do you think it's dangerous?'

'Of course,' I said. 'Most alien things are.'

'Not all of them,' said Penny, pressing my arm against her side. 'Have you really never seen anything like this before, Ishmael?'

'Not like this,' I said.

'Then what are we going to do?'

'It's a hole,' I said. 'So the only logical next step is to look into it.'

Penny snatched her arm free and gave me a hard look.

'Ishmael, you are not seriously thinking of putting your head in there? That would be like sticking your head in the lion's mouth!'

'You can keep hold of my belt,' I said. 'Make sure I don't fall in.'

'Ishmael! This is a seriously bad idea, and you know it!'

'It's a hole,' I said reasonably. 'How else can I find out what's inside?'

'At least, put your hand in first! For all you know, we could be looking at the blackness of outer space and there's nothing in there but cold vacuum.'

'I'll hold my breath,' I said. 'You hold my belt. You'd better use both hands.'

She stepped behind me, thrust both hands up under my jacket, and took a firm grip on my belt with both hands. I took a careful step over the safety line, leaned forward, and extended my right hand. It was still a few inches away from the dark surface when an unseen force grabbed hold of my hand and jerked it forward. My hand plunged into the darkness and disappeared, without leaving a single ripple on the surface of the hole. My arm suddenly appeared to end at the wrist. The unseen force was still pulling, but I dug my feet in and held my arm where it was.

I couldn't feel anything inside the hole. I tried to wiggle my fingers, but I couldn't even get a sense of where they were in relation to my hand. I moved my wrist left and right across the surface of the hole, but I still couldn't feel a thing, not even a sense of movement. I began to get a horrid feeling that the hole had taken my hand, eaten it right off, so there was nothing left beyond my wrist . . . and that was why I couldn't feel anything. I jerked my hand back out. It took some strength to overcome the force trying to pull me in, but my hand emerged from the flat dark surface entirely undamaged. And when I stepped back from the hole, the sense of the pull disappeared.

I flexed my fingers. It was as if they'd never been gone. There was no feeling of pins and needles, no sense of returning circulation after numbness. I rubbed my hands together, and they both felt exactly the same.

'Not cold, or hot, or anything,' I said to Penny. 'Keep a tight hold on my belt.'

And before I could think better of it, I leaned forward and thrust my head into the hole.

The light cut off immediately. There was nothing but a

darkness so absolute it was far more than just the absence of light. I couldn't see or hear or feel anything. I tried to say something just to hear my own voice, but I had no sense of where my mouth was or even how it worked. Then something hauled me back, and my head came out of the hole again. Light filled my eyes, and all the sounds of the world returned. I took a deep breath and smiled at Penny.

'I'm all right. I'm fine. Why did you pull me out?'

'You weren't moving! I was worried. Well? What's in there?'

'Nothing,' I said. 'Nothing at all. Do you want to try?'

She smiled dazzlingly. 'Of course!'

Her belt didn't look that strong, so I took a firm grip of her hips with both hands as she leaned forward and stuck her head through the dark surface of the hole. I felt the unseen force jerk her forward, as if trying to pull her out of my grip, but I held on tightly, making sure only her head went in. Seeing her neck end abruptly at the dark surface was really disturbing. I gave her a count of ten, and then pulled her back out. Penny shook her head slowly, as though to make sure it was still properly attached.

'You're right, Ishmael, there's nothing in there. But it was weird . . . I didn't even feel like I needed to breathe.' She stopped, frowned, and looked back at the hole. 'Do you suppose the missing archaeologist could still be in there, somewhere?'

'Depends how far down the hole goes, and what's at the other end,' I said. 'Conditions at the top of the hole could be very different from what's at the bottom. Come on, let's go talk to the nice scientists. See what they can tell us about the hole.'

We set off down the hill. The Professor saw us coming, at last, and called for her people to stop work and take a break. They all insisted on finishing what they were doing, but eventually they gathered together outside the equipment centre, presenting a unified front to the outsiders. The Professor introduced us, and the first of the scientists to smile and offer his hand was Terry Crane. Tall, gangling and almost aggressively cheerful, he wore a battered sweater and jeans under his anorak.

'So, what do you think of the hole? Isn't it just the most amazing thing you've ever seen?'

'Doesn't it scare you?' said Penny. 'It's already swallowed up one person.'

'I know!' said Terry. 'That's what makes it so fascinating!'

'We don't let Terry get too close to the hole,' said the Professor. 'He's prone to sudden enthusiasms. This is Robert May.'

Robert was a sturdy medium-height young man with a neatly trimmed beard and practical but expensive clothes. He nodded brusquely, and didn't offer to shake hands.

'What's your area of expertise?' I said.

'Communications,' he said flatly. 'But I haven't been able to detect anything coming out of the hole. This equipment is barely adequate, and being cut off from the rest of the scientific community isn't helping. Before they'd let me get in the car to come here, they took away my laptop and my phone! And then they have the nerve to get upset at our lack of results. It's almost as if they want us to fail . . .'

'Stick to the facts, Robert,' said the Professor.

'We've sent all kinds of transmissions into the hole,' said Robert. 'But there's never any response. Any recording equipment we drop in doesn't work, and doesn't come back. It won't be long before we're reduced to throwing in handwritten notes, begging someone on the other side to talk to us.'

'Robert is our resident pessimist,' said the Professor.

'Somebody has to be,' said Robert.

The young woman standing next to him introduced herself as Ellie Garland. A surprisingly glamorous creature, given the setting and the company. Tall and waif-like, she wore smart but casual clothes under her anorak, making them look stylish just because she was wearing them. She had long flat blonde hair, pale-blue eyes, and a smile that never really got beyond polite. She looked like a catwalk model's idea of a scientist.

'My speciality is theoretical physics,' she said, in a calm soft-spoken voice. 'And this is the point where I usually drop the magic word "quantum" and everyone stops asking me questions. I've been trying to work out how the hole is able to exist in our world, given that just by being what it is it's defying a whole bunch of fundamental laws.'

Paul Osborne was pale-skinned and dark-haired, and didn't

smile or offer to shake hands when the Professor introduced him. He seemed almost studiedly anonymous in his look and his clothes, and the Professor had to prompt him to explain what he did.

'It's my job to work out how the hole affects living things,' he said, in a quiet uninflected voice, as though he could barely be bothered to answer. 'I'm in charge of the test animals.'

'And you killed all of them,' said Penny.

'There's no evidence they're dead,' Paul said calmly. 'They just didn't come back after we put them into the hole.'

'Why would whatever's in the hole want to take your animals?' said Penny.

'Perhaps whatever is on the other side is building a collection. Perhaps that's what the hole is for – to acquire specimens for examination.'

'Like the missing archaeologist?' I said.

'Exactly,' said Paul. 'He could be the first human being to visit another world. Don't you envy him?'

'Depends on the other world,' I said. I looked at the other scientists. 'Is that the consensus? That the hole is actually a tunnel to somewhere else?'

'The mathematics support it,' said Ellie.

'This is why I keep saying we need to send in a human subject!' said Terry, almost bouncing up and down in his enthusiasm. 'Someone who can report back on what's actually going on inside the hole!'

'You are not going in, Terry,' the Professor said firmly. 'It's far too dangerous, and there's no guarantee we could get you back safely.'

Terry shrugged. He seemed quite used to having his sudden enthusiasms shot down.

The final member of the team had been staring coldly at Penny and me through all of this. A tall skinny presence with a permanent scowl, a rough sweater and jeans, and far too much nervous energy. The Professor introduced him with a sigh, as if performing a regrettable but necessary task.

'This is Michael Lee. Call him Mike, he hates being called Michael. A child prodigy at mathematics, he was allowed into Cambridge University at far too young an age, which is probably why he still has difficulty getting on with people. He's the smartest one here, and never lets us forget it. Thinks he knows everything, but has a hard time proving it to anyone who doesn't speak fluent numbers. This is his first time as part of a field team, and from the way he's been acting almost certainly his last. Don't take any crap from him. We don't.'

'It's my job to think outside the box,' Mike said loudly. 'To see the things that everyone else misses. It was my idea to dig the tunnel, to prove the hole didn't penetrate into the hill.'

'You still had to get someone else to dig it for you,' said Robert.

Mike ignored him, his gaze fixed on me. All of the team were in their twenties, but Mike was clearly the youngest. I got the feeling he would always be the youngest in any scientific gathering, and would always hate it. He stuck his chin out, like a defiant child.

'I just want it on record that I object to their presence here.'

'What record?' said the Professor.

Mike's scowl deepened. 'You know what I mean. We don't need Government snoops peering over our shoulders, watching everything we do, getting in our way and interfering with our work.'

'You mean getting in the way of you doing whatever you feel like doing,' said Robert.

'Exactly!' said Mike. 'That's what science is about.'

'I don't have a problem with a Government presence here,' said Robert. 'That could prove useful if something goes wrong.'

'Like what?' said Mike.

'What if the hole starts growing and doesn't stop?' said Robert. 'What if Ellie is right, and the hole is a tunnel to somewhere else and something comes out of it?'

'And you think I'm paranoid!' said Mike.

'You are,' said Ellie.

'We need someone official here, on the spot, to make important decisions in case of an emergency,' said Robert.

'Like shutting us down before we've finished our work?' said Mike.

'We're not in charge here,' I said. 'Penny and I are just security.'

'You think someone's going to steal the hole?' said Ellie.

'We're here to make sure no one bothers you, or the hole.'

'You're just here to keep an eye on us!' said Mike.

'Of course,' I said. 'Any reason why we shouldn't?'

'Why should we trust you,' Mike said flatly, 'when the Government doesn't trust us?'

I could see the idea taking root among the others. The Professor rushed into the sudden silence.

'Let me remind you, we're only here because the Government is funding this investigation,' she said sternly. 'We're all being very well paid for our efforts, and we have to accept their terms of engagement when it comes to the hole. Also, their restrictions on who we can talk to about it. Given that the hole has already killed one person, we need some security. If nothing else, we don't want some outsider strolling in and getting hurt.'

'Who's going to come here?' said Mike. 'We're miles from anywhere civilized.'

'And yet the archaeologists just happened to dig in the one place where the hole turned up,' I said.

'And why did the farmer come here with his metal detector?' said Penny. 'Does the hole attract people? Draw them in like bees to a flower? Or flies to a flytrap . . .?'

The team looked at each other.

'I haven't detected any emanations from the hole,' said Robert.

'The hole is interesting,' said Mike, 'but I wouldn't call it attractive.'

'None of my test animals showed any interest in the hole,' said Paul. 'Right up to the point when I lowered them in.'

'But there is a fascination to the hole,' said Ellie. 'Now we know it's here, we can't stop thinking about it.'

'Well, of course!' said Terry. 'Because we've never encountered anything like it.'

'The hole, or whatever it really is, doesn't belong here,' said Ellie. 'It doesn't obey any of the rules of our world. I think it's something from outside, grafted or superimposed on to our reality by forces beyond our understanding.'

'That would imply purpose,' Terry said carefully. 'That the hole was put here for a reason.'

'Yes,' said Ellie.

'That has yet to be established!' said Mike.

'Nothing has been established so far,' said Robert. 'Or at least nothing useful. We've been able to prove the hole isn't all sorts of things, but not what it is. Never mind what it might be for.'

'All the more reason to have security here,' said the Professor. 'To keep us safe while we work.'

'But that's not why they're really here, and you know it,' said Mike. 'The Government doesn't trust us to tell them everything we learn here.'

'And just possibly, they don't want any of us being tempted to sell those secrets to a foreign power,' said the Professor.

She stared meaningfully at each member of the team in turn. None of them said anything, but they all got the point. There was an awkward silence, only broken when Terry launched into another of his enthusiastic outbursts.

'Look! I volunteer to go into the hole. I'll attach a steel cable to my belt, so I can be hauled back at the first hint of trouble. We need to know what's going on inside that hole.'

'Don't keep asking, Terry!' said the Professor, rubbing tiredly at her forehead. 'My answer isn't going to change.'

'None of the test animals I put into the hole ever came back,' said Paul.

'They died, just from being inside the hole?' said Penny.

She gave me a hard look, and I knew what she was thinking: *I can't believe we put our heads in there!*

'We don't know the test subjects are dead,' the Professor said carefully. 'Every time we tried to haul them out the steel cable broke, so we couldn't reclaim them.'

'It didn't break,' Mike said flatly. 'It was torn.'

'Either conditions inside the hole are too much for the steel cable, or someone on the other side doesn't want to be disturbed,' said Robert.

'I could wear a two-way radio,' said Terry. 'One of those military jobs we were given for secure communications. I could be in constant contact from the moment I enter the hole.'

'That's enough, Terry!' said the Professor. 'All right everyone, back to work. You've met the security people and had your say, but that's not going to get us the answers we need. Remember, we're on the clock.'

The team broke up and went back to their own particular pieces of equipment. They didn't talk to each other. It didn't look to me like they were working as a team; more like they were only concerned with their own separate agendas. I looked at the Professor and she nodded briefly, anticipating my question.

'They prefer to stick to their own areas of expertise, and I've decided that's the fastest way to get results. Keep them in competition with each other.'

'Is there anything in particular you'd like us to do?' I asked.

She lowered her voice, again not nearly as much as she thought.

'If the hole really is a tunnel . . . Could you stop something from the other side coming through?'

'Have you seen anything?' said Penny.

'No,' said the Professor. 'But I can't help feeling we're stuck here with a door we can't close and God knows what's on the other side.'

'What makes you think a visitor would automatically be dangerous?' I said.

'Can we afford to assume it won't be? Given that the hole is completely alien to everything we know . . . How could whatever made it have anything in common with us?' The Professor looked back up the hill at the hole and suddenly shuddered. 'There's no reason why invaders should come in shiny metal ships. Perhaps they prefer to sneak in through the back door. We have to be prepared. For anything.'

'Why would aliens want to invade us?' I said. 'To blow up our cities, steal our oceans, have their wicked way with our women? If the laws of physics are so different where they're from, why would they even want to come here?'

'Because no matter who or what you are,' the Professor said steadily, 'in the end it always comes down to the need to expand your territory. Are you armed?'

'No,' I said.

'I asked for armed support!'

'If anything should happen to make that necessary, I can always call some in,' I said. 'For the moment, all we have is a hole that someone might have fallen into accidentally. Don't let your imagination run away with you, Professor.'

'Take it easy, Ishmael,' said Penny. 'She's scared.'

'Of course I'm scared!' said the Professor. 'Faced with something I don't understand that may actually be impossible for the human mind to comprehend . . . Looking into that impossible darkness is like looking into Hell. I wish I'd had the guts to tell the Colonel to go to hell. Do we have to wait until people start dying before you take the situation seriously?'

I met her gaze squarely. 'I assure you, Professor, I am taking this very seriously. The hole suggests all kinds of possibilities, good and bad. But there's no evidence yet of any real danger.'

The Professor turned her back on us and strode into the equipment centre to join her people. Who might or might not have overheard everything we'd been saying. The Professor peered over their shoulders, studied readings, made pertinent suggestions, and generally irritated the hell out of all of them.

'Ishmael, why are we here, exactly?' said Penny. 'Did the Colonel give you any special instructions?'

'Just to keep the hole safe from outsiders and protect the team,' I said. 'And if necessary, protect the team from the hole.'

'What if we have to protect the world from what's inside the hole?' said Penny. 'Come on, Ishmael. If there's one thing we can be certain of, it's that aliens are real.'

'And that's all we know,' I said. 'So let's not panic ourselves just yet.'

'When I looked at that hole,' Penny said steadily, 'the darkness reminded me of my bedroom as a child after my father put the light out. That kind of darkness could contain anything. Anything at all.'

'There weren't any monsters then,' I said. 'And the odds are, there aren't any now.'

'But monsters are real,' said Penny. 'We've faced enough of them.'

'It's always people who do the most evil,' I said. 'They can be worse than monsters.'

Penny smiled wanly. 'If you're trying to reassure me, you're doing a really awful job.'

'Let's go for a walk,' I said. 'Take a look at our surroundings.'

We wandered off across the great grassy slope of the hill, giving all our attention to the countryside spread out before us. The day was heading into evening, but there was still enough light to see by. It was very quiet and very peaceful, and the open hill fell away before us like a great green waterfall.

'All this open space is a good thing,' I said finally. 'No one is going to be sneaking up on us.'

'Until it gets dark,' said Penny. 'I think it could get really dark here really quickly. There were no lights on the road, and the nearest town is miles away.'

'I'd still be able to see or hear anything coming,' I said. 'In such a deserted location, any change is bound to stand out.'

Penny frowned suddenly. 'It is very quiet though, isn't it? I mean, why aren't there any birds singing? Or insects buzzing? Could something have frightened them away? And why can't we hear any traffic from the road? Has word got around that it isn't safe to drive here once it starts getting dark?'

'You're thinking about the Beast again, aren't you?'

'Aren't you?'

'Every area has its own version of that story,' I said. 'And the few times I've been sent to investigate, it's always turned out to be just another local legend – apart from the time it was two guys in a phosphorescent pantomime-horse costume. I took a good look around as we were walking up the hill. There are no animal tracks anywhere.'

'Hold it!' said Penny. 'No signs of any local wildlife. Isn't that unusual in itself?'

'Yes,' I said. 'It is . . .'

Suddenly there was uproar behind us. People yelling, back at the site. I looked round to see the Professor and her team running towards the hole. I ran to join them, sprinting up the hill, with Penny pounding along behind. As I got closer, I could see the steel cable unspooling from the great steel drum, stretching out as it disappeared into the hole. It was moving at some speed, as though it was plunging deep into the hill. I caught up with the Professor, already breathing hard as she fell behind the others.

'What is it?' I said. 'What's happened?'

'It's Terry! He hooked himself up to the cable, sneaked past us, and jumped into the hole. I told him not to!'

'Didn't anyone notice?' said Penny, as she caught up with us.

'We were busy!' said the Professor.

I ran on, leaving both of them behind, and joined the rest of the team as they stood before the hole. Staring helplessly as the cable disappeared into the darkness.

'He isn't just falling,' said Robert. 'He's moving too quickly for that.'

'And the speed is increasing,' I said.

'You can't tell that just from looking!' said Mike.

'Listen to the cable and the drum,' I said.

The taut cable thrummed as it shot into the dark surface of the hole, while the engine on the drum made loud sounds of strain. Penny and the Professor joined us, breathing hard from the climb. The Professor struggled to get words out.

'The radio . . . Terry said he'd take . . . a radio in with him.'

Robert reached inside his jacket and brought out a military item. 'Terry, this is Robert. Can you hear me? Talk to me, Terry.'

We all waited, but there was no response. I looked at the Professor.

'Stop the cable. Have the drum's engine pull him out of there.'

She nodded quickly to Paul. 'Do it. Bring the young fool back.'

'The cable's moving at too great a speed,' said Paul. 'If I just hit the brakes, the cable could snap. It's broken before inside the hole.'

'It didn't break, it was torn,' said Mike.

'Not now, Mike!' said Ellie. 'We have to get Terry back.'

'If the cable snaps, we could lose him,' said Robert.

I grabbed hold of the steel cable with both hands and clamped down hard. The racing steel rasped loudly against my bare flesh, but I could feel the cable slowing. I piled on the pressure, and the cable ground to a halt. I looked at Paul.

'Stop the engine. Pull him back.'

'Do it!' said the Professor.

Paul ran down the hill to the drum, while I kept up the pressure on the cable, clamping my hands down hard. Paul hit the brake and then sent the engine into reverse, and the cable slowly began to emerge from the hole. I let go, and stepped back. Penny grabbed my hands, and made me show her my palms. They weren't even reddened from the friction.

'That's not possible!' said Robert. 'The strain should have torn your skin apart . . .'

'I'm a trained field agent,' I said.

I've used that line before when people catch me doing things people shouldn't be able to do. It doesn't actually mean anything, but it seems to satisfy people. Everyone stopped looking at me, and went back to watching the steel cable as it slowly reappeared from the hole's darkness. Winding itself back on to the drum, foot by foot. There was no sense of resistance from the other end. I leaned in close to study the cable, but the steel seemed entirely unaffected by its time inside the hole. Robert was still trying to reach Terry on his radio. There was no answer.

'There's no guarantee Terry is still on the other end,' said Mike.

'Shut up, Mike!' said Ellie. 'Just for once, shut up. You're not helping.'

When the last of the cable emerged from the dark surface of the hole, Terry was still attached. Ellie started to cry out his name, and then broke off as Terry dropped to the ground. The cable dragged his limp body across the grass, bumping and jerking, until Paul shut down the engine. Terry lay still. I knelt down beside him and tried for a pulse, even though I knew I wouldn't find one. Ellie started forward, and the Professor grabbed her arm.

'Ellie, don't.'

'Help him!' Ellie said loudly. 'We have to help him!'

'I'm sorry, Ellie,' said Robert. 'He's beyond helping.'

'He's dead,' I said.

The Professor glared at me. 'I told you something like this would happen!'

I rolled Terry over on to his back. There were no obvious wounds or injuries, or any clear cause of death. But his face was contorted into an expression of utter horror.

TWO
Something in the Dark

It's never easy when someone you know dies.

You feel like something hit you hard, knocking all the strength out of you. All the scientists wanted to do was stand there and look, hoping that if they just gave the world enough time it would realize this was wrong and put things right. Which is why it helps to have someone like me around, who's seen more than their fair share of dead bodies and is ready to make all the necessary decisions for you.

'The hole is now officially off limits to everyone,' I said. 'At least until we have some idea of what happened here.' I turned to the Professor and said her name loudly until she looked at me. 'What do you want me to do with the body, Professor Bellman?'

She looked at me blankly. 'What?'

'Terry's body,' I said patiently. 'We can't just leave him lying here.'

'Why not?' said Mike. 'Isn't this a crime scene? You're not supposed to interfere with a crime scene.'

'This is a secured area,' I said patiently. 'Which means normal rules don't apply. We can't call the police, because they're not supposed to know things like the hole even exist. I'm not even sure a crime has been committed. Terry took it on himself to jump into the hole without telling anyone. But we do need to put his body somewhere secure until I can contact someone higher up for instructions.'

I looked at the hole, and the dark circle stared back like a great unblinking eye. It had to have taken a lot of courage for Terry to go into the dark on his own. Unless something in the hole called to him, overwhelming his common sense. Not for the first time, it occurred to me that there had to be a lot more to the hole than met the eye. I realized the others were looking at me, and quickly took up my train of thought again.

'Technically, Terry didn't actually die here, but inside the hole. So there is no crime scene. I'll settle for preserving whatever evidence there may be on the body. Professor, where do you want me to put Terry?'

She didn't seem to know what to say. She just looked from the corpse to the hole and back again, as though hoping one of them might provide an answer. I looked at the scientists, standing huddled together like sheep in a storm. None of them seemed in any condition to make a decision.

'There are always the tents,' said Penny.

I nodded to her thankfully. I can always rely on Penny to be practical when things get emotionally complicated.

'I'll put Terry in one of the tents,' I said. 'And then that will be off limits as well. Would any of you like to help? He was your friend.'

No one volunteered. Ellie turned her head away, as though she couldn't stand to look at the body any more. The Professor extended a comforting hand to her, but Ellie turned to Robert, who put an arm around her shoulders. He couldn't seem to take his eyes off the body. Mike looked at Ellie and Robert, but said nothing. I couldn't read the expression on his face, but I didn't think it had anything to do with Terry's death. Paul looked lost: like he wasn't sure what he should be feeling or doing. Robert suddenly realized he was still holding his radio. He looked at it, as though wondering whether he might still hear something from Terry, and then put the radio away.

I knelt down, took a firm hold of Terry, and then straightened up again. The dead always seem to weigh a lot more than the living, but I'm stronger than I look. Penny stepped forward and carefully removed the steel cable still attached to Terry's back. Luckily it was just a simple clamp, snapped on to the back of Terry's belt. It was a good thing the belt hadn't snapped when he was hauled back so abruptly. If it had, he would have been lost in the dark for ever and we would never have known what happened to him.

Like the archaeologist who disappeared into the hole.

Terry hadn't thought nearly enough about safety precautions

before he made his great jump into the unknown, but that seemed typical of the man. Sudden enthusiasms, that was what the others said. And this one got him killed. I headed down the hill to the tents on the far side of the site. Penny walked beside me, and the others trailed along behind. None of the scientists had anything to say, which struck me as a little odd. By now shock should have started giving way to tears, hysteria, fond memories of the man. Anything that offered the promise of comfort. But instead they just trudged silently along in the rear, as though they were part of a formal procession. The scientific mind, I supposed. Think now, feel later. Penny moved in beside me.

'So what do we think? Did Terry jump, or was he pushed?' she said quietly. 'Was this suicide, death by misadventure, or murder?'

'Depends whether anyone else was involved,' I said, just as quietly. I wasn't concerned the others might overhear us: we've spent so much time working together we can understand murmurs no one else could. 'You yourself saw . . . No wounds on the body, no obvious cause of death. It could be that conditions at the bottom of the hole were simply too extreme for his mind to cope with. That would explain the look on his face.'

Penny shuddered briefly. 'What could he have seen that was so bad it scared him to death? We didn't see anything.'

'I don't know,' I said. 'Perhaps whatever lies at the bottom of the hole is beyond human understanding. Or endurance.'

'I can't believe Terry would do something so stupid,' said Penny.

'I've been wondering whether someone else encouraged him,' I said. 'For reasons of their own.'

'Or pushed him in when his nerve failed,' said Penny. 'And now they're afraid to admit it.'

'Or maybe this was just cold-blooded murder,' I said. 'Someone struck Terry down, attached the cable, and threw him in. Taking advantage of Terry's previous enthusiasm to muddy the waters.'

'Who'd want Terry dead?' said Penny.

'If we knew why, we'd probably know who,' I said. 'All

we really know about these scientists is what they've chosen
to show us. There could be all kinds of emotional entangle-
ments we know nothing about.'

'All of the scientists were working together in the equipment
centre,' said Penny. 'Wouldn't they have noticed if another
person went out, as well as Terry?'

'Would they?' I said. 'Apparently no one noticed Terry
sneaking around in the background.'

'So what do you think really happened?' said Penny.

'I don't know,' I said.

We finally reached the cluster of little tents. I stopped in
front of the nearest one, and Penny undid the flaps for me.

'Hey!' Robert said suddenly. 'That's my tent!'

'He's got to go somewhere,' said the Professor.

'But . . . it's my tent,' said Robert.

I looked back at him. 'Anything in there you don't want
me to see?'

Robert shook his head. He still had an arm around Ellie,
but only in an absent-minded way. He wasn't even looking at
her any more. I carried Terry into the tent, while Penny stayed
outside, guarding the entrance. There was nothing inside apart
from a brand-new sleeping bag, left half-open to air. It didn't
look like anyone had used it yet. I laid Terry down beside the
bag, unzipped it all the way, and then manhandled the body
into the bag with as much dignity as possible, under the
circumstances. I tucked Terry in neatly, and then zipped the
sleeping bag all the way up to his chin, so only his head was
left showing. Partly to help preserve any evidence there might
be on his body, and partly to discourage the body from getting
up and walking about. I've seen stranger things, and I had to
wonder whether the Terry who'd come out of the hole was
the same Terry who'd gone in . . . I stood over him for a long
moment, trying to understand the look on his twisted face.
Fear, horror, revulsion . . . What could he have seen in the
hole, or beyond it? What could he have found, deep in
the darkness, that just the sight of it was too much for him to
bear?

I looked around the tent. Only a little of the evening light
made its way through the open flaps, but I could see clearly

enough in the gloom to be sure there were no personal belongings and no luggage. Nothing for me to search or examine. So I left the tent, closed the flaps, and turned to confront the waiting scientists.

Penny was still standing guard, carefully positioned between the scientists and the tent. They were huddled closely together, comforting each other with their presence. Reminding themselves that at least they weren't alone in this. Robert and Ellie were holding hands now, like lost children. Mike stood on Ellie's other side, as close as he could get. She didn't seem to notice. Paul was staring at the tent, but I doubted that was what he was seeing in his mind's eye. The Professor seemed lost in her own thoughts. I cleared my throat to draw the scientists' attention, and everyone's gaze jumped to me, desperate for answers or guidance I didn't have. So I just stared back at them.

'We need to follow protocol on this,' said Penny, to fill what was threatening to become an awkward silence. 'Professor, you need to contact whoever is supervising this investigation and tell them to send more people to secure the area.'

'And that they need to take away the body and arrange for an autopsy,' I said. 'Give us a better idea of exactly what happened to Terry.'

'We're not allowed to call out,' said the Professor. 'For security reasons. They confiscated all our mobile phones before they put us in the cars that brought us here.'

Penny looked at Robert. 'But you have radios. You used one to try to reach out to Terry . . .'

'They're only for on-site use,' said the Professor. 'If you try to call out, the frequency is blocked.'

'Same with the laptops they provided,' said Robert. 'We can only access information on agreed sites. And no email.'

'Then how are you supposed to tell anyone that you have an emergency and need assistance?' I said.

'I asked the Colonel that,' said the Professor. 'He said "Don't have an emergency!".'

I nodded. That sounded like the Colonel.

Penny frowned. 'But there must be a Government contact, as well as the Colonel . . .'

'Black Heir is in charge of site security,' said the Professor.

She stopped for a moment, as she saw me react to the name. I knew Black Heir, and not in a good way. I nodded for the Professor to continue.

'We're only allowed to talk to Black Heir. The Colonel said he would be too busy dealing with the bigger picture.'

'Whatever that means!' said Mike. He looked at me challengingly. 'Do you know what that means?'

'No,' I said. 'The Colonel doesn't talk to me about things like that.'

I turned to Penny. 'He doesn't normally work alongside Black Heir . . . They're supposed to cover an entirely different territory from the Organization.'

'What do you mean, different territory?' Mike said suspiciously. 'And what kind of a name for a Government department is Black Heir? I never heard of them. What's their purpose, their remit, their authority?'

'I asked the Colonel that,' said the Professor.

'And?' said Robert.

'I was told "Don't ask!",' said the Professor.

'Oh . . .' said Mike. 'One of those departments.' He seemed strangely satisfied to have his suspicions confirmed.

'If Black Heir is involved, there's more to this situation than we're being told,' said Penny.

'Wouldn't be the first time,' I said. I turned back to the Professor. 'Who do you talk to at Black Heir?'

'A Mr Carroll,' she said. 'I don't know him.'

She looked at the scientists, but they all shook their heads.

'Who actually assembled this team?' I said. 'Carroll or the Colonel?'

'I did,' said the Professor. 'According to the Colonel's specifications. I was told to put forward the names of suitable people, based on their published work.'

'But you must have some way to contact this Carroll when you have important results to report,' said Penny.

'He calls us once a day, at eight a.m.,' said the Professor. 'He isn't due to talk to us until tomorrow morning. You're the security expert, Ishmael. You must understand how these things work.'

I just nodded, not committing myself. One of the reasons I prefer working for the Organization is that they usually keep this kind of bullshit to a minimum. Departments like Black Heir are never really happy unless they're overcomplicating the situation.

'Why are we being kept so isolated?' said Mike. 'Don't they trust us?'

'It was made very clear to me that I shouldn't ask awkward questions,' said the Professor. 'And when it came to Black Heir, I got a definite feeling I was better off not knowing.'

There was general nodding among the scientists. They were still too shaken to get properly angry.

'Terry and his tent are off limits to everyone,' I said. 'So please give it plenty of room.'

'What if we want to pay our respects?' said Ellie.

'Terry will understand if you leave that till later,' I said.

'Why are you so determined to keep us away?' said Mike, scowling. 'What are you afraid we might do if we did have access to him?'

'I don't know,' I said. 'And I have no intention of finding out the hard way. There's nothing any of you can do to help Terry except leave him in peace.'

Robert looked at what used to be his tent. 'Where am I going to sleep now?'

'You can sleep with me,' said Ellie.

'You were going to anyway,' said Mike. He glared round at the others, as they looked at him. 'What? It's not like I'm telling tales out of school. We all know those two are together.'

Ellie didn't even look at him. She was staring at the tent like a child confronted with a house that might be haunted.

'What if . . . What if Terry gets up and starts walking about?'

I looked at her curiously. 'You think that's something he's likely to do?'

'I don't know!' said Ellie. 'You saw his face . . . Who knows what he found or what found him on the other side of the hole . . . What he was exposed to in there, or what it might have done to him.' Her shoulders slumped suddenly, and all the fire went out of her. 'I wish I'd never heard of the hole. I wish I'd never come here.'

'Even if he did get up again, it's only Terry,' said Mike. 'And he wouldn't hurt a fly. You know that, Ellie.'

There was more nodding among the scientists. They all seemed to relax a little. Ellie smiled at Mike, and he smiled back.

'You always know the right thing to say, Mike, when it matters,' said Ellie.

'Doesn't make up for what he says the rest of the time,' said Robert.

'Let's move away from the tent,' Penny said diplomatically. 'I think we'll all feel better and think more clearly once we've put some distance between us and the body.'

They all liked the sound of that. The Professor led the way back up the hill, and the scientists were only too happy to follow. Penny and I hung back, so we could talk quietly again.

'You don't really think Terry might start stumbling around the camp, do you?' said Penny.

'Doesn't seem likely,' I said. 'You don't make zombies by accident, it takes a lot of hard work. But I zipped him in really tightly, just in case. He'll have a hard time working the zip from inside the bag. Of course, he could end up humping across the grass like a giant caterpillar . . .'

'Oh, ick!' said Penny.

We went to join the others, who had come to a halt outside the equipment centre. Proximity to the scientific instruments seemed to help reassure them they were still living in a sane and rational world. I gave their equipment a cursory glance, as if I knew what I was looking at.

'Did any of your instruments show anything out of the ordinary before Terry went into the hole?'

They all shook their heads quickly. To make it clear that whatever had happened, it had nothing to do with them.

'So!' I said sharply, and everyone jumped just a little. 'Question. Did Terry go into the hole of his own accord, or was he pushed?'

The question seemed to catch all of them by surprise. Some actually looked shocked at the very idea that Terry's death could be anything other than a tragic accident. It was also clear they didn't want to have to take the idea seriously, but now the question had been raised they couldn't stop thinking about it. The Professor looked at me accusingly.

'Why would you say something like that? Terry was always talking about the need for someone to go into the hole and observe conditions directly, instead of studying it remotely through the instruments. He didn't trust the readings we were getting, and sometimes I don't think he even trusted the equipment. You were there when he volunteered to go in and I turned him down. Perhaps I should have put my foot down harder . . .'

Mike scowled at me. 'Are you suggesting someone pushed Terry in? That's insane! Why would you even think that?'

'I'm security,' I said calmly. 'It's my job to think things like that and then question people like you about it. Did any of you see anything out of the ordinary before Terry went into the hole?'

The scientists looked at each other uncertainly, searching their colleagues' faces for anything they might be holding back, but no one had anything to say. They all looked more confused than anything. In the end, the Professor spoke for all of them.

'All of my people were intent on their instruments. I was there in the equipment centre with them, giving all my attention to the team and encouraging them to work harder.'

'Being your usual pain in the arse,' muttered Mike. The others pretended not to have heard that.

'You said Terry went off on his own, Professor,' said Penny.

'That's right,' the Professor said quickly. 'He said he was going to the toilet. We have a portable cabin, out beyond the tents. He didn't need permission to go; Terry was just one of those people who always feel the need to announce their toilet breaks. I didn't think twice about it. He must have known I wouldn't, and took advantage of it. Because he knew that if I'd even suspected what he was planning, I'd have stopped him. The first any of us knew what was happening was when we heard the cable unwinding from the drum. By the time we looked round, it was already too late.'

'We all saw the cable moving,' said Paul. 'But it took us a moment to realize what that meant.'

'I told Terry not to do it!' said the Professor. 'You all heard me! Why didn't he listen to me?'

'That was typical of Terry,' said Mike, surprisingly kindly. 'You know what he was like. Once he got an idea into his head, there was no shifting it.'

Everyone was nodding. They all had some kind of smile on their face, remembering Terry in better times.

'I think I was the first to realize what the moving cable meant,' said Robert. 'I ran straight to the hole to try to stop Terry.'

'Why didn't you just hit the brakes on the drum?' said Penny. 'That would have stopped him in his tracks before he could reach the hole.'

'I didn't think of it,' said Robert. 'I should have, but all I could think of was the hole.'

'We all went running up the hill to the hole,' said Ellie, patting Robert reassuringly on the arm. 'But when we got there, Terry was gone. There was just the cable diving into the hole. We all arrived together. No one was there on their own, and no one could have helped Terry. It must have been his idea . . . None of us would have wanted to hurt Terry, everyone liked him.'

'Well . . .' said Robert.

'Yes?' I said.

'I don't want to speak ill of the dead, but Terry could be a bit wearing.'

Robert looked around, to make sure he wasn't speaking out of turn, and when no one objected he carried on.

'Too much enthusiasm, no matter how well meant, is bound to get on your nerves after a while. But no one ever raised their voice to him. Well, not much.'

'Who raised their voice to Terry?' said Penny.

'We all did,' said Mike. 'At one time or another. We all liked the man, but there's no getting away from the fact that he could be a real pain. He was one of those people who . . . when they have what they think is a brilliant idea just won't shut up about it. You heard him arguing with the Professor and not listening to what she said. We all knew he'd raise the subject again, no matter how many times he got shot down.'

'But no one ever lost their temper with Terry,' said Ellie. 'You couldn't. It would have been like kicking a puppy.'

'Did he make any enemies while he was here?' I said, looking searchingly from one face to another.

'We haven't been here long enough to make enemies,' said the Professor. 'And anyway, we've all been working too hard.'

'Have there been any serious arguments?' I said patiently. 'Any disagreements that got out of hand?'

'We argue all the time,' said Paul, not quite condescending as he explained the way of the scientific world to an outsider. 'We're always disputing theories, or the best way to prove them. That's what we do. It's never personal.'

'It's always about science,' said Robert. 'Never about us.'

'Except when it is,' said Mike.

The others all looked at him, and he stopped talking.

'All of you stay here,' I said. 'I want to take another look at the hole.'

No one objected. They didn't look like they wanted to go anywhere near the hole ever again. I walked back up the hillside, with Penny at my side. She didn't ask why I wanted to look at the hole; which was just as well, because I didn't have an answer. Except that it seemed far more likely I'd get answers from the hole than from the scientists. I stopped short of the hole, well behind the safety line, and Penny and I studied it in silence for a while. It looked just as it had before. Like someone had dropped a freakishly large inkblot on the hillside.

'The Colonel was right,' I said finally. 'This hole is unnatural. Just by being here, it's an insult to the natural order of things.'

'I hate the way it just sits there,' said Penny. 'Not reacting to us at all, like we don't matter. I feel like throwing things at it, just to get a response.'

'We can do that after we've tried everything else,' I said. 'For now, let's concentrate on what happened to Terry. I'm wondering whether he might already have been dead before he went in. Whether the look on his face was caused by his murder, and nothing to do with what's inside the hole. Could someone have killed him and then just used the hole to dispose of the body?'

'There were no wounds on the body and no obvious cause of death,' said Penny. 'I suppose we could be talking poison . . . But what would be the motive? And even if he was murdered in some way yet to be established, how could any of the scientists have sneaked away to dispose of the body without being noticed? Or are we thinking that one or more of the scientists were in collusion with the killer?'

We both looked back down the hill at the scientists. They'd gone back into the equipment centre to check their instruments, carrying on with their work as though nothing had happened. Or possibly to take their minds off it.

'I don't know that I'm suggesting anything just yet,' I said. 'Nothing about this case makes any sense.'

'What if this is just what it appears to be?' said Penny. 'A scientist who didn't think things through and got himself killed.'

'The Colonel only assembled this team and sent us here because an archaeologist disappeared into the hole,' I said. 'And now we have another death. Maybe the hole does attract people to it, with some kind of hypnotic summons they don't even know they're hearing.'

'Can you hear anything?' said Penny.

I listened carefully. I could hear the scientists talking quietly together, and the sounds their machines made. I could hear the familiar comforting sounds of Penny's breathing and heartbeat. But I couldn't hear anything out in the gloom gathering around the campsite, and I couldn't hear anything coming out of the hole. I shook my head.

'Nothing out of the ordinary. And nothing even remotely suspicious.'

'Then maybe it was an accident,' said Penny. 'Just because we're here doesn't automatically mean there are suspicious circumstances. People die in accidents all the time.'

'But why did Terry die so soon after you and I got here?' I said. 'That has to be suspicious. Could he have been intending to tell us something, about the hole or the team, that someone couldn't risk us knowing? Or did the hole want to show us what it could do?' I glared at the unresponsive circle and it stared steadily back at me; dark and silent, giving nothing away. I shook my head angrily. 'I can't believe I only just got here and someone has already died.'

'It wasn't your fault, Ishmael,' said Penny.

'No,' I said. 'It wasn't. But I will find out whose fault it is, and make them pay.'

I turned my back on the hole and strode off down the hill. Penny had to hurry to keep up with me. I crashed to a halt outside the equipment centre and rattled the clear-plastic wall to get their attention. They didn't want to leave their work until they saw the look on my face, and then they reluctantly emerged from the centre and stood before me like sulky children assembling before a teacher. They looked like they expected me to have everything worked out by now, so I distracted them with more questions. Starting with the Professor, because she was looking the most impatient.

'How exactly did you assemble this team, Professor Bellman? Why these particular people to investigate this phenomenon?'

'I only supplied a list of names,' she said flatly. 'Someone else made the final decision. The Colonel, or possibly someone from Black Heir . . . I have to say, I'm surprised how little you seem to know about this operation. Weren't you properly briefed before you set out?'

'The Colonel only ever tells me what he thinks I need to know,' I said. 'And when a case is as urgent as this one, sometimes not even that.'

'Who is this Colonel?' Mike said suspiciously. 'Are we under military control? No one said anything to me about working for the military! I thought we'd been brought here in the cause of pure science. Not so our findings could be weaponized.'

'If you had known, would it have stopped you?' said the Professor.

'Well, no,' said Mike. 'I wasn't going to miss out on a chance to work on something like this. But I would have asked for more money.'

'There is no pure science any more,' said Ellie. 'Not as long as the Government and the military control all the funding.'

'I'm still not sure what this Colonel has to do with anything,' said Robert.

'He's in charge of this operation,' said the Professor. 'But Black Heir is in charge of site security. That's why we report to Mr Carroll. Don't make more of this than it is, Mike. We're here because we're experts in the field.'

'We're not in a field,' said Mike. 'It's a hill.'

Ellie hit him in the shoulder. 'Idiot!'

Everyone still had some kind of smile on their faces.

'I'm here because of my theoretical work,' said the Professor. 'I gather there weren't many other theorists to choose from. That's why they put me in charge. But if I'm honest, everyone else here is way ahead of me.'

The team exchanged looks behind her back, the kindest of which was condescending. Apparently all of them had decided the Professor was well past her sell-by date. But they were all careful to have politely expressionless faces when she glanced back at them.

'Are all of you familiar with the Professor's work?' I said.

'Of course!' said Ellie.

'Most of it,' said Paul.

'Ground-breaking stuff, for its time,' said Robert.

'Of course the maths,' said Mike, 'has come a long way since then.'

The Professor glared at me. 'Look, you're wasting time trying to find connections between us. We all met for the first time when we arrived here. Delivered in separate cars, by security drivers who'd been ordered not to talk to us. We're all strangers to each other, though I suppose we all know each other's published work. We have no reason to be enemies.'

But I'd already noticed the looks passing between Robert and Ellie and Mike. Enough to make it clear they had known each other before, and not in a good way. I let that go for the moment and looked around the team, not singling anyone out.

'How were you approached to join this operation?'

One by one, they admitted they weren't exactly sure who'd picked them. It was just an authoritative voice on the phone, offering them a once in a lifetime opportunity to do significant cutting-edge work. They were persuaded by the offer of generous research grants, and threatened with expulsion from their universities if they didn't cooperate. When pressed, they all reluctantly admitted this voice knew things about their past that no one else should have known. The looks on their faces made it very clear they weren't about to share those things with me, no matter how hard I pressed them.

'Isn't that how you security people usually operate?' said Mike, accusingly.

'No,' I said. 'That's not the Organization's way. But it does sound a lot like Black Heir. Which is one of the reasons why I don't work for them anymore.'

'Of course not,' said Mike. 'You're the good cop. We're supposed to trust you and open up. Right?'

'Don't push him, Mike,' said Ellie. 'Who knows what he's capable of?'

'We weren't told what we would be working on till we got here,' said Robert. 'Just that it lay within our areas of expertise.'

'No one mentioned the hole,' said Paul.

'Probably didn't want to frighten you off,' said the Professor.

'Oh, come on!' said Ellie. 'If I'd known about the hole, you couldn't have kept me away with a loaded gun.'

'The hole is a game changer,' said Robert.

'For science?' said Penny.

'For everything,' said the Professor. 'Even the most basic understanding of this hole will make all our careers.'

'Assuming we're ever allowed to talk about it,' said Mike.

'Well, yes,' said the Professor. 'There is that.'

Penny broke in, fixing me with a hard look. 'I don't think we can afford to wait for the early morning call, Ishmael. Use your phone and call the Colonel. The Organization needs to know what's happening here.'

'Don't you think we can cope?' I said. 'Solving murders is what we do.'

'Terry's death wasn't a murder!' said the Professor.

'It's a suspicious death,' I said. 'And Penny and I have a lot of experience when it comes to investigating such things.'

'It was an accident!' said Robert.

'Was it?' said Ellie. 'I wish I could be sure of that. You saw the look on his face . . .'

'Whether this is a murder or not, we can handle this,' I said.

'This isn't about Terry's death,' Penny said steadily. 'It's about the hole. We've never encountered anything like this before.'

'It's just another mystery,' I said.

'Wait a minute!' said Mike. 'I think we're missing something here. What is this Organization you keep talking about?'

'A private security group,' I said smoothly, 'that specializes in cases of the weird and uncanny.'

'You get a lot of those?' said Paul.

'You'd be surprised,' I said. 'Or you would if you were allowed to know about them. Now, you've spent the last fourteen hours studying the hole. What do you think it is?'

They all but fell over each other in their eagerness to explain what they thought and defend their various theories. They didn't quite shout each other down, but it came close. It quickly became clear they weren't prepared to accept even basic common ground, and none of them would back down. Careers were on the line, as well as egos. Things were threatening to get out of hand, until the Professor intervened and shouted them all down. The scientists subsided, reluctantly, and allowed her to take first crack at explaining the hole to Penny and me.

'I still maintain the hole is a natural phenomenon,' the Professor said carefully. 'A repeating event, brought about by a rare combination of circumstances. Something that comes and goes, that exists on the very edge of what we're capable of understanding. Just as I described in my original papers, all those years ago. Fashions in science come and go, but maths is still maths, and my equations are still sound. I believe holes like this have been appearing and disappearing all over the world throughout recorded history. Holes in the world, for people to fall through. Such things could be responsible for all kinds of disappearances – everything from the *Mary Celeste* to the Bermuda Triangle.'

The team looked at each other, but had the good manners not to laugh out loud.

'The hole is really just the entrance to a tunnel,' Ellie said firmly. 'A connection between this world and another one. And, of course, any entrance can also be an exit. Things from this other world could have passed through previous tunnels and emerged into our world. Giving rise to all kinds of stories – everything from the Yeti to the Loch Ness Monster. Creatures that don't fit into our natural order of things, because they were the product of completely different conditions.'

Mike started his explanation the moment Ellie finished, but Robert talked right over him.

'The hole is a space/time anomaly,' he said loudly. 'An extraordinarily rare quantum event. What we see when we look at the hole is just our minds doing their best to interpret a weak spot in reality itself; where two universes have slammed up against each other and the walls have worn thin, producing an opening. What's on the other side of the hole couldn't hope to exist here. It's not just another world we're talking about, but another reality.'

Ellie hit him with a really cold look. 'Just because the maths allows for the possibility of something doesn't make it inevitable. This hole is so unlikely, it has to be a manufactured event. A door opened from the other side. The tunnel has to be of extraterrestrial origin, and quite possibly an invasion point. I'm not the only one to think this. Why else are the Government and the military so concerned?'

Nobody actually disputed what she was saying, but they all looked like they wanted to. And that they were getting just a bit tired of Ellie insisting they were in danger from alien invaders. Just like they'd got tired of Terry and his enthusiasms . . . Penny gave me a quick look and mouthed the word 'alien', but I just shook my head slightly. It wasn't like I had anything useful to contribute on the subject.

'You're all wrong,' Mike said bluntly. 'And overcomplicating things, as usual. The hole is what's left over from some secret Government project. An attempt to open a dimensional doorway that went seriously wrong. That's why they feel the need for so much security. In fact, it wouldn't surprise me if we were put here to help cover it up, as much as investigate it.'

'You're the one who's overcomplicating things!' said Paul. 'The hole is really just the equivalent of a spy camera, a way for somewhere else to study conditions in our world. They can't come through themselves because they couldn't exist under the physical laws that make up our reality. We're in no danger, it's just a spy hole.'

'So, if they're looking down a microscope at us . . .' said Mike. 'If we're nothing more than bugs to them, what will happen if they decide to fumigate the place?'

'An alien invasion is an alien invasion, no matter where it's coming from,' Ellie said stubbornly.

'It would seem the only thing we can agree on is that the hole is an opening of some kind,' said the Professor. 'It might pose a threat, or it might not. We need to do a lot more work before we can be sure of anything.'

'I say we should block up the hole, plug it up,' said Ellie.

'If we leave it alone, it will disappear of its own accord,' said the Professor.

'But if the hole is artificial,' said Mike, 'and someone on the other side is watching us, this time the hole could be here to stay. Now they've found something worth watching.'

Nobody liked the sound of that. They started to stir unhappily, so Penny decided it was time to distract them again.

'Robert, Ellie and Mike,' she said. All three of them looked at her sharply, and Penny smiled sweetly. 'It's obvious the three of you have some history from before you were brought here. So how do you know each other?'

They looked at each other and then looked away quickly, just a bit guilty at having been caught out. Paul and the Professor seemed honestly surprised. Apparently they'd been so caught up in their work they hadn't noticed. Robert looked at Ellie, who looked at Mike, who didn't want to look at either of them. All three clearly wanted to stubborn it out, but I just let the silence drag on until they felt they had to say something, rather than just stand there and be stared at.

'Mike and I used to be an item,' Ellie said reluctantly. 'When all three of us were in the same year at Cambridge.'

'We were very happy together,' said Mike.

'You were,' said Ellie. 'And then I met Robert, and I left Mike to be with him. We moved to Oxford, while Mike stayed at Cambridge.'

'And we never saw each other again until we wound up here,' said Robert. 'Something of a shock for all of us.'

'I thought Mike was going to have a heart attack!' said Ellie. 'Is it my fault you never got over me, Mike?'

'I thought I was coping really well,' said Mike. 'That I was getting on with my life. Until I saw you again, and realized I hadn't had a life since you walked out on me. I'd just been marking time, burying myself in my work. You ruined my life.'

'You always were too ready to blame the world for problems of your own making,' said Ellie.

'But I've been entirely professional ever since I arrived here!' said Mike. 'I've never once let my emotions interfere with my work.'

'You still should have said something,' said the Professor. 'Why didn't any of you say anything?'

'Because it wasn't anyone else's business,' Robert said stiffly. 'We came here to work, that's all. Even though Mike has spent most of his time arguing with my theories and interfering with my work, just to impress Ellie.'

'That's not true!' said Mike. 'You're the one who's been getting in everyone's way and refusing to listen to anyone else.'

'And you're always so ready to support Ellie,' said Robert.

'Because she's right.' Mike turned to Ellie, his face flushed. 'Tell him! Tell him I've been nothing but professional!'

'I don't believe Mike has allowed his emotions to get in the way,' said Ellie. But she didn't look at him as she said it.

'You told me you'd seen Mike going off on his own to have a good cry behind the tents,' said Robert.

Ellie scowled at him. 'You didn't have to tell them that!'

Mike looked at Ellie as though she'd betrayed him, then his mouth firmed and his eyes went cold. 'You were never worth crying over, Ellie. And Robert never had a good idea he didn't steal from someone else. Like he stole you from me.'

Robert stepped forward, his hands closed into fists, and Mike went to meet him. I stepped quickly in between them.

'None of that matters!' I said loudly. 'What's important is the hole, and Terry's death.'

'You're quite right, of course,' said the Professor. 'But really, what can we do for Terry? He's beyond anyone's help. The best thing we can do for him is get back to work and try to reach a better understanding of what killed him.'

'What do you believe should be done about the hole, Professor?' said Penny.

The Professor carefully avoided looking at Penny, or me. 'It's not my job to decide things like that.'

'I thought the Colonel put you in charge,' I said.

'You heard the young geniuses,' said the Professor. 'My work is out of date, I'm just here to organize things . . . I think we should take a break, and have something to eat and drink. There's tea and coffee, and things in cans.'

The scientists stirred uneasily. They glanced at the tent I'd put Terry in, and then looked quickly away. When people are confronted with death, they often feel it's wrong to carry on with the everyday things of life because the one they've lost can't do so. They'd get over it. I looked thoughtfully at the Professor. There was something she wasn't telling me.

'The Colonel must have expected you to contribute something,' I said.

'I am here to evaluate the team's ideas,' said the Professor, just a little testily. 'I oversee their work, decide who should be encouraged, who is wasting time . . . Who gets first shot at the best equipment and most access to the hole, depending on how much I approve of the direction their work is taking—'

'But you only listen to people when their theories agree with your old work,' said Mike. 'If any of us has the nerve to challenge that, we get pushed to the back of the queue. If you'd listened more to Terry, we could have set up a safe experiment for him. He wouldn't have felt the need to jump in blindly. He might still be alive if you'd let us supervise him.'

'If he'd just done as he was told, he'd still be alive!' said the Professor.

'So the team's progress was dependent on impressing you,' said Penny, refusing to be sidetracked.

'Well, yes . . .' said the Professor.

'So which theories do you support?' I said.

'I believe the hole to be the scientific equivalent of an act of God,' the Professor said coldly. 'Beyond our understanding.

The best we can hope to do is observe what it does and contain it until it inevitably disappears.'

'The hole can be understood,' said Robert. He'd been itching to break in, and started talking the moment the Professor stopped. 'We may not be able to figure out why the hole appeared, but we should be able to work out how it's able to maintain itself here. It's just a matter of observation and deduction.'

'Exactly,' said Paul. 'We're not students, Professor. We know what we're doing.'

'I've already told you what the hole is for,' said Ellie. 'And what might be coming through it. We should concentrate on stopping that.'

'Hush!' said Paul. 'They might be listening.'

Ellie shot him a withering glare, but he didn't seem too bothered.

'Of course you want to believe these things,' said the Professor, not quite sneering at her own team. 'Your careers, your futures, depend on solving this. You're all so young . . . You think if you hit an unexplained phenomenon hard enough, it'll have no choice but to reveal its secrets. You think you can force the universe to make sense. But that's not how things work. I used to think like you, but look at me now – yesterday's news. And your future, my children.'

'Tweeds?' said Mike. 'I'd rather die.'

Penny spoke up again, determined to get the conversation back on course. 'You've all explained your own theories, but what did Terry believe?'

There was a pause. The scientists looked inquiringly at each other, and then appeared somewhat taken aback when it became clear none of them knew.

'We never really listened to him,' said Ellie.

'Terry was always the practical one,' said the Professor. 'He never advanced any theories of his own that I can recall. Terry was always busy looking for hard evidence to back up or disprove other people's ideas. He made himself responsible for overseeing the lowering of equipment and animal test subjects into the hole. The animals were always a lot calmer when he was around. They liked Terry. We all did. Though he had become increasingly frustrated that all his hard work wasn't producing any answers.'

'He used to swear something awful, every time the cable came back out with a broken end and nothing on it,' said Mike.

'He needed to prove his worth to the team,' said Ellie. 'To prove that choosing him hadn't been a mistake. That's why he was so keen to go into the hole himself.'

'But what made him decide to do it despite the Professor's firm instructions?' said Penny.

'I think that was down to you,' Robert said flatly. 'The moment you arrived, he knew he had to impress you. And through you, impress the people in charge. So you could say you're responsible for his death . . .'

'It's my responsibility to keep you alive,' I said steadily. 'But I can only do that with your cooperation. So from now on, it's important that all of you listen to what I say and do what I tell you.'

'What has that got to do with Terry's death?' said Mike.

I met his gaze squarely. 'A jump into the dark without proper preparations was never going to end well. Not when so many things had already failed to come back. I need all of you to treat the hole with more respect. It's not just your pet science project, it's a killer.'

The Professor and her team stared silently back at me, their expressions bordering on mutinous. The hole was their toy, to play with as they chose, and they weren't going to let me take it away from them.

'All right,' I said. 'Let's look at this another way. Whichever of you could best demonstrate they understood the hole would be the winner in this little game of yours. Rewarded with big Government grants, the applause of your peers, and probably exclusive access to any future holes. This isn't a team, Professor. It's a contest.'

The scientists looked at me pityingly, amazed it had taken me so long to work out something so obvious.

'Academia is a jungle, red in tooth and claw,' said Mike, 'where only the strongest can hope to survive.'

'But that means all of you had a reason to kill Terry,' said

Penny. 'You all needed to be first to the truth if you were
going to win the big prize. By going straight to the source,
by taking a shortcut, Terry cheated.'

'The thought never entered our minds,' Robert said flatly.

'We all liked Terry,' insisted Ellie. 'He was hard-working,
always helpful, always funny . . . He did all the shit work no
one else wanted to do and never complained once.'

'He was the best of us,' said Mike, unexpectedly. 'He had
the nerve to go head to head with the hole, instead of just
studying it from a safe distance.'

I decided I'd pushed this as far as I could for the moment. I
looked around the campsite. The shadows were taking over, as
the last of the light went out of the day.

'It'll be dark soon,' I said. 'You've all worked long enough
for one day, and you've been through a lot. The Professor is
right, take a rest. Tired people make mistakes, and that can
be dangerous.'

'Exactly,' said the Professor. 'Shut it all down, people, and
call it a day.'

One by one the scientists nodded and went back into the
equipment centre. I looked at the Professor as a thought
struck me.

'What's powering your equipment? I haven't noticed a
portable generator anywhere.'

'It's tucked away behind the tents,' said the Professor. 'Solar-
powered and very quiet. Because we're not supposed to mess
with the environment or upset the neighbours. Even though
there aren't any. Now help me set up the perimeter lights.
Because once night falls, it's going to get really dark around
here.'

Setting up the perimeter lights turned out to mean walking
round the camp turning on the powerful lights already set in
place and adjusting them until their bright illumination covered
every part of the site. Penny and I did all the work, while the
Professor stood back, telling us what to do and raising her
voice when we got something wrong. I found this quietly
amusing, Penny less so. The extra illumination made no difference at all to the hole, with not even a hint of reflection on

its flat black surface, but the hole had extra lights to make sure it was covered from every direction. By the time we were done, the campsite was almost fiercely lit and the growing dusk outside the camp seemed even darker in comparison.

Robert and Paul set up a small camp fire at the centre of the site, and we all arranged ourselves round it. They'd made a surprisingly efficient job of it, for two theoretical scientists. The flames crackled loudly in the quiet, spreading a cheerful warmth. A small pile of gathered branches stood to one side for future fuel. The evening was growing steadily colder as darkness fell, and everyone had their hands outstretched to warm them at the flames.

'You'd think the Government could have provided us with a proper heater,' said Mike. He seemed almost pleased to have something new to complain about. 'Instead of all this boy-scout nonsense.'

'This is fun,' said Ellie. 'I like this. It's not often a city girl like me gets to sit round a camp fire at night.'

Robert looked at her. 'I never knew you wanted to.'

'You never asked,' said Ellie.

Mike smiled quietly, as though he'd just achieved some small but significant victory over his rival.

'At least the fire should discourage any of the local wildlife from sneaking up on us,' I said.

'Though I still haven't spotted any,' said Penny.

The Professor and her scientists looked vaguely out into the darkness around them. It wasn't something they'd thought about.

'I suppose there's always the Beast of Brassknocker,' Mike said lightly.

'Don't, Mike,' said Ellie. She snuggled up against Robert, and he put his arm round her. 'The fire's nice, but I've never spent a night outdoors before. I don't think I feel safe without walls to protect me . . .'

'I'm here,' said Robert. 'I'll take care of you.'

Mike looked like he wanted to say something, but didn't.

The Professor had placed an old-fashioned kettle directly on the burning branches, and we all watched it impatiently, waiting for it to sing. A few wisps of steam curled unhurriedly from its spout.

The Professor sniffed loudly. 'We're here to solve one of the great mysteries of our time, and they couldn't even give us proper supplies! I know this was all put together in a hurry, but have you seen the coffee and tea? Cheap supermarket own-brand stuff. But it'll be hot and wet, so we'll have to settle for that.'

'I thought there was supposed to be better stuff on its way?' said Paul. 'We were promised . . .'

'I'll believe it when I see it,' said Mike.

'Good food and drink are necessary for good work,' said the Professor. 'Feed the body and you feed the mind.'

'Right,' said Mike. 'I am feeling distinctly underappreciated.'

'Never knew you when you didn't,' said Robert.

'There are cans,' said Paul.

'I am *not* eating cold baked beans,' said Mike, just a bit dangerously.

'Stick the can in the fire,' said Paul.

'Oh, dear Lord!' said Mike, lowering his head into his hands. 'Has it come to this . . .'

We all sat quietly for a while, watching the dancing flames and waiting for the kettle to boil. It took its own sweet time, just to make us appreciate it, but eventually we all had a plastic cup of something hot in our hand. Mike started to put forward his theory about the hole again, in even more detail, but the Professor shot him down.

'The day is over, Mike, let it go. Ishmael is right, tired minds rarely produce anything worth listening to. I suggest we all retire to our tents and get some sleep. We started far too early in the morning, and if nothing else we need to be up bright and early for Mr Carroll's eight a.m. call.'

Robert looked at the tents unhappily. 'I don't know how I'll get any sleep, with Terry that close to us.'

'You can hold on to me, dear,' said Ellie.

Robert smiled at her and hugged her to him. Mike looked at them, and then looked at the fire.

But it turned out no one was ready to go to bed just yet. It was too early, and their body clocks wouldn't cooperate. Talk moved around the fire in fits and starts, going nowhere, until Ellie finally said what everyone was thinking.

'Who can sleep after everything that's happened? How can we get any rest with the hole just up the hill? Anything could come out of it in the night, while we're asleep and defenceless. We should put up a barricade of some kind.'

'All we have is the wood we gathered earlier for the fire,' said Mike. 'And I am not going out into the dark to look for more. And let's face it, anything powerful enough to create a tunnel between two worlds would be able to smash through any barricade we could put up.'

'You can all sleep soundly,' I said. 'Penny and I will stay on guard and keep watch till morning.'

Penny looked at me. 'It was good of me to volunteer, wasn't it?'

'I thought so,' I said.

Time passed. No one seemed to feel much like talking, but no one wanted to go to their tents. Night had fallen, and there was nothing outside the site's circle of light but an impenetrable darkness. It occurred to me that looking at the night was very like looking at the hole. Equally unknowable, and potentially equally threatening. But it was all very quiet, with not even a breath of wind. Penny and I shared a look, and then moved around the circle on our own, sitting and talking quietly with people. I needed them to open up while they were tired and their defences were down. There might or might not have been a murder, but I still needed to know as much as possible about these people.

Penny had always been better at this part of the job than me. She had the human touch, which I still sometimes lacked despite all my years of living among people. I sometimes wonder if I'm just playing at being human, and deep inside I might still be something else. There have been times when I've looked into my mirror and just for a moment thought I saw something else looking back at me.

Sometimes in my dreams I catch glimpses of a nightmare place, alien and awful. And part of me wants to call it home.

Since I don't have Penny's conversational skills, I mostly concentrate on being a good listener. Somewhat to my surprise, this worked really well with the Professor. She'd added a little something to her tea from an engraved silver hip flask, and she leaned in really close so she could speak confidentially.

'Retirement is breathing down my neck,' she said. 'I've been clinging on to my university post by my fingernails for years, riding the reputation from my old work. Giving long-winded lectures to bright young minds so much smarter than me. Pretending I'm still capable of contributing anything of value. When the Colonel approached me, I jumped at the chance to lead this team. Though of course I was careful not to let him know that.

'This is my last chance to be involved with work that matters. The field might have left me behind, but if I can guide this team to important discoveries I can still ride their coat-tails to glory. Go out with a bang, with one last triumph. I think I deserve that, for all the long years I've put in. For having a career instead of a life.'

I watched Ellie talking to Penny, on the opposite side of the fire, in a voice so quiet no one but me could have heard. Ellie wasn't snuggling up to Robert any more, and when she looked into the fire her gaze was disturbed and distracted, and just a bit lost.

'I think I might have made a mistake, leaving Mike for Robert,' she said quietly to Penny. 'Robert is strong and reli-able, someone I can depend on. I thought that was what I wanted. But Mike . . . could always make me laugh. Make me try new things, make me feel alive. I thought I saw maturity in Robert, but really . . . a lot of the time he's just boring. I know I'm not being fair to him . . . but even though Robert and I are the same age, he always feels so much older.

'And if I'm honest . . . I'm smarter than he is. Sometimes I can feel myself holding back, hiding that from him, so he won't feel overwhelmed or threatened. I never felt I had to do that with Mike. He could be proud of me. Robert does love me, I've never doubted that; but sometimes love isn't enough. Is it wrong of me, to want to be happy no matter who it hurts?'

'Does Mike know you feel like this?' said Penny.

'He's been trying to win me back ever since we got here,' said Ellie. 'Just by being there, being supportive. Being himself. Yes, I know, he can be irritating. That's just because he thinks so quickly and says things before he can stop himself. But at least I can be sure he's always thinking of me; while Robert often seems far too willing to lose himself in his work.'

It must have been a night for confessions, because while all that was going on, Robert was opening up to me.

'I'm so scared I might be losing Ellie,' he said, staring into the fire. So he wouldn't have to look at me, or Ellie. 'I don't know what I'm doing wrong, but I can feel her drifting away. I try to be strong for her, to be someone she can always lean on. But more and more she seems . . . distracted, restless, as though she needs something I don't know how to give her.'

He looked up suddenly from the fire to glare at Mike. 'Look at him. Cocky little bastard. I never liked him. Always has to prove he's right, and everyone else is wrong. I was so happy when Ellie chose me over him. And now . . . She can't leave me! She just can't. I don't know what I'd do without her.'

After a while I went and sat with Mike, and he couldn't wait to unburden himself to me.

'So it's my turn now, is it?' he said. 'I've seen you and Penny moving round the circle, getting everyone to open up to you. Well, why not? It's not like I'm ever going to see you again after this. And sometimes you can say things to a complete stranger that you couldn't say to anyone else. My big secret? My career is going nowhere, so I have to win this little contest and prove I'm right about the hole. I was a child prodigy, you see, and they always burn out quickly. I'm still turning out good work and making sure it's published in all the right places. Publish or perish . . . In the academic jungle, you're constantly having to prove your right to be there. But it's been years since I produced anything to equal the first great blaze of my early work. Frankly, I was surprised they wanted me for this team. I wouldn't have chosen me. But since they were dumb enough to ask, I was dumb enough to say yes. I didn't need to be bribed or threatened. I wanted this.

'And . . . it's only by winning this battle of theories that I can be sure of getting Ellie back. She's never had any time for second best. That's why she left me for Robert. Not because he was better than me, but because his career was going places and mine wasn't. But I've been listening to Robert's ideas about the hole and he is way out of his depth, even if he won't admit it. I can win this. I have to, so Ellie will come back to me.'

Penny did her best to get Paul talking, but he didn't have much to say. He didn't seem to believe anyone could be interested in him. And when she finally ran out of leading questions, he started asking questions about Penny and me.

'You work so well together,' he said. 'I'm impressed. You're so efficient in everything you do, at getting answers to questions the rest of us haven't even thought to ask. It never even occurred to us that what happened to Terry might not have been an accident. Though I think it probably was. He was desperate to achieve something, so scared we'd see him as superfluous. We should have told him how helpful he was. How much he contributed to the team. I think that would have meant a lot to him.'

Outside the camp's circle of light there was nothing but the night. At least there was a half-moon, and a sprinkling of stars. When Mike pointed this out to Ellie, she found it fascinating. Living in the city, she'd never seen anything like it. Possibly because it never occurred to her to look up. She wanted someone to point out the various constellations to her, and was disappointed when no one could. Apparently, it wasn't anyone's area of expertise.

'Come on, people,' the Professor said finally. 'It's time all good little scientists were tucked up in their sleeping bags and getting their heads down. Some of you are falling asleep where you are.'

They all got to their feet, yawning and stretching, then laughing quietly as they caught yawns from each other. Everyone said their goodnights, and headed for their tents. Mike watched Ellie go off with Robert until both of them disappeared into the one tent, as if trying to convince himself Ellie might change her mind at the last moment. When she didn't, his shoulders slumped. The Professor turned suddenly to Penny and me.

'You know, Paul and Mike could always double up, so you could have a tent.'

Mike and Paul looked at each other, and it would have been hard to tell which of them was more appalled at the prospect.

'No need for that,' I said kindly. 'Penny and I will sit guard until it's light. Then we'll wake some of you up, and you can take over so we can get a few hours' sleep before the eight a.m. call.'

'Suit yourselves,' said the Professor. Paul and Mike quickly disappeared into their tents, before anyone could change their minds. The Professor still hesitated. 'I can't decide what I should tell Mr Carroll. Hopefully something that won't get us shut down. Terry's death was unfortunate, but the hole is important. We can't abandon it because of one stupid accident.'

'They won't remove you,' I said. 'If only because they couldn't hope to get another qualified team here before the hole disappears. You're all they've got.'

The Professor nodded slowly, not entirely convinced, and went to her tent still frowning.

Once everyone had settled down for the night, it was a lot quieter. The only sounds were the quiet crackling of the flames, as wood stirred and shifted in the fire. I fed it a few more branches. Penny warmed her hands at the leaping flames. I didn't. She suddenly smiled at me.

'You don't feel the cold, do you? Even after all this time, it's the little differences that still catch me by surprise. Though I have to say, bringing that steel cable to a halt with your bare hands was really impressive.'

'I don't like to do things in public that make me stand out and might make me memorable,' I said. 'But it was necessary. I had to try to save Terry.'

She could hear the self-reproach in my voice and leaned in close beside me, pressing her shoulder against mine. 'You did your best, and it was more than anyone else could have done. The moment Terry decided to go into the hole, it was too late to help him. Like jumping a man with a gun and hoping it isn't loaded.' She looked up the hill. 'That hole really does give me the creeps, Ishmael. What do you think it is?'

'Ellie's idea is probably closest,' I said. 'It has to be a gateway to somewhere else. And given the look on Terry's face, not anywhere we'd want to go.'

'We didn't see anything when we stuck our heads in,' said Penny.

'Terry didn't stop at the top,' I said. 'Who knows what there might be all the way down at the bottom of the hole.'

Penny shuddered briefly. 'It's getting seriously cold. Maybe we were wrong to pass up on a tent.'

'Someone has to stand guard,' I said. 'I could do it on my own, but I'm not sure you'd be any safer inside one of those tents. With no way to see what might be sneaking up on you. No way to defend yourself from something that's crawled up out of the hole, or some scientist who feels like wandering around with malice in mind.'

'You know, you worry me sometimes,' said Penny. 'The way you think. Don't you trust anyone here?'

'Do you?' I said.

'I asked you first.'

I looked across at the tents. 'I don't see any clear motive for Terry's murder. But there's a lot about this situation I don't understand.'

'About the hole?' said Penny. 'Or the people?'

We sat together for a while, in companionable silence. It was very quiet, and very still. I couldn't hear anything moving anywhere in the site. All the perimeter lights seemed to be operating at full capacity. Penny stirred uneasily, and scowled around her into the darkness.

'I'm still not hearing any wildlife,' she said. 'You'd think something would be out and about by now. Foxes, badgers, maybe an owl.'

'Or perhaps the legendary Beast,' I said.

'Don't even go there!' said Penny. 'That's all we need right now, more complications. Unless . . . Do you think the Beast's appearances could be linked to the hole's coming and going?'

'I'm not ready to rule anything out,' I said. 'But the Beast is just one of many old stories and legends associated with Brassknocker Hill that might or might not have something to do with the hole.'

'Such as?' said Penny. 'Come on, Ishmael, you can't just drop a conversational bombshell like that and then walk away from it.'

'This whole area has an abnormally high number of stories about people who go missing for no good reason and are never heard of again. I suppose the best known is probably the one about a young man, some centuries back, who left his family cottage to go out into a winter's night. He had to do some necessary chores, or check the livestock. Nothing he hadn't done a hundred times before. But he hadn't been gone long before the family heard him cry out, in shock and horror. He started to scream, but his scream was cut short.

'When the family rushed outside, he was gone. Even though there was nowhere for him to go. The open field stretched away before them, all the way to the horizon, covered in a thick layer of snow, gleaming brightly under a full moon's light. The young man's footsteps stood out clearly in the snow, heading across the field. And then, they just stopped. There was no sign of any struggle, or any footsteps in the snow other than his. He was just gone.'

'What happened to him?' said Penny.

'Nobody knows,' I said. 'Perhaps he found a hole. Or it found him. Most of these old stories have no proper ending. They're just cautionary tales. Like the local legends about a headless dog called Old Black Shuck, which haunted back roads and chased sinners to drag them down to Hell.'

'A headless dog?' said Penny. 'How does it smell?'

'How do you think?' I said, and we laughed lightly together.

'The Beast . . .' said Penny. 'Could it be something that comes out of the hole, from some other place, and then disappears back into it? After it's done what it was sent to do? That would explain why there's sometimes such a long gap between its appearances.'

'There are no records of the Beast killing people,' I said. 'Only livestock.'

'But it does leave claw marks on doors, from where it's tried to get into houses,' said Penny. 'Perhaps it's looking for living specimens to take back with it. To be experimented on . . .'

'You're determined to scare yourself, aren't you?' I said.

'Scary tales around a camp fire are traditional,' said Penny. 'And I'm not really scared, because I have you. I'd back you against any monster of the night.'

'Because I'm not human?' I said.

'Of course you're human! Human is as human does. I'd back you in any situation because you're smarter than any monster, and I trust you to kick its arse no matter what it is. Now, assume there's no Beast. Assume someone here is responsible for Terry's death, and only used the hole to dispose of the body in order to muddy the waters . . . Who do you think the murderer might be?'

'I don't know,' I said. 'It's hard to get any traction in this case, when all we have is a body. No clues, no obvious cause of death . . . No clear motive, and no alibis to challenge. No one will admit to noticing anyone else leaving the equipment centre after Terry; and they all arrived at the hole together, after he'd gone in. I can't even be sure there is a killer. The more I think about it, the more inclined I am to take Terry's death at face value. He said he wanted to jump into the hole, and he did. If there is a killer here, it's the hole.'

'There are some motives,' said Penny. 'Take the love triangle between Robert, Ellie and Mike. Lot of harsh emotions going on there.'

'But how could their love triangle lead to Terry's murder?' I said.

'I don't know,' said Penny. 'Maybe he saw or heard something he shouldn't have? Though that could apply to anyone. What if someone here isn't who they're supposed to be, and Terry found out? Maybe some foreign power wanted to steal the secrets of the hole and sent a spy to infiltrate the group? No, I think it's something to do with the love triangle.'

She suddenly stopped and looked at me. 'I just find it so sad that two people fell in love and thought it was for ever, only to find it wasn't. I don't want something like that to happen to us, Ishmael.'

'Hey, hey . . .' I said. 'Where did that come from? What makes you think anything's going to go wrong between us?

We're not part of any triangle. Unless you've been seeing the Colonel on the side . . .'

'Idiot!' she said, smiling. 'No, it just made me think about my parents. I grew up with Mummy and Daddy quarrelling all the time. And there are just so many things that separate you and me. You told me you haven't aged a day since you first appeared in this world, back in 1963. You won't grow old, but I'm going to. So will you still love me when I'm sixty-four?'

'I love you, now and for ever,' I said. 'Believe me, I have no intention of ever leaving you.'

'But you'll have to eventually,' she said. 'Or to be more exact, I'll have to leave you. Because even after I'm dead you'll still be here.' She laughed briefly. 'You know, other people don't have conversations like this.'

'Probably just as well,' I said.

And then we both looked round sharply. Something was moving, out in the night. Hidden in the darkness beyond the camp's circle of light. We both got to our feet and quickly looked around. The darkness threw back my gaze almost contemptuously, and whatever movements Penny and I had heard had stopped.

But there was still something out there. I could feel it looking back at me.

'I definitely heard something,' Penny said quietly. 'What did you hear?'

'It might have been footsteps,' I said, not taking my eyes off the dark.

'Human?'

'Maybe.'

'Could it be one of the scientists moving about?' said Penny, glancing back at the tents.

'Why wouldn't they announce themselves?' I said. 'And besides, I didn't hear any of the tent flaps being undone.'

We both broke off, as we heard something moving again. The sounds seemed heavier, more deliberate this time. As though they wanted to be heard. Prowling around the perimeter of the camp, but never entering the light. Drawing closer and then falling back. Taunting us. I still couldn't get any sense of what was out there. Just a presence in the night.

'That's not the local wildlife,' I said. 'It sounds large. Heavy.'

'Human?' Penny said again.

'I don't think so. There's something wrong . . . about the way it moves.'

'You think it's a threat?'

'Why else would it be hiding in the dark?'

Penny caught her breath. 'Could it be the Beast?'

'I can't see anything,' I said. 'It's too dark out there, even for me. Maybe if I shut off all the lights, my eyes would adapt.'

'Don't you dare!' said Penny.

We both stood very still, listening hard. Whatever it was moved slowly along the perimeter. I turned slowly, following the sounds, trying to get a fix on where it was. The sounds stopped, abruptly. I was listening so hard now that Penny's breathing and her racing heartbeat were almost deafening.

'I'm not seeing anything,' said Penny, after a while. 'Is it still out there, standing still, watching us? Or could we have scared it away?'

'It's still there,' I said.

'Could it be the Beast?' said Penny, lowering her voice to a whisper.

'Stay here,' I said. 'I'll go out there and take a look.'

'Are you kidding me?' Penny said fiercely. 'I'm not staying here on my own while you go strolling off into the night to face God knows what! You're not going anywhere without me.'

'Then stick close,' I said.

'Should we take a burning branch from the fire?' said Penny.

'I wouldn't advise it,' I said. 'Out there in the dark, the light would make you a target.'

Penny glanced at the fire, and thought better of it. I strode across the camp to the nearest perimeter and stopped at the furthest point the light could reach. I stared out into the darkness. I can usually see something, no matter how dark it gets; but out in the countryside, with hardly any moon, it was like looking at a featureless black wall. There were no more sounds and no movements. I couldn't even get a sense of something out there.

'It wanted us to know it was there,' I said quietly. 'It made those sounds deliberately. So why is it being quiet now?'

'Maybe we scared it away,' said Penny.

'I don't think it's scared,' I said.

A scream broke the silence, from the direction of the hole. A very human scream, cut suddenly short. I turned and sprinted up the hill, heading for the hole. I could hear Penny pounding along behind me, but I couldn't slow down to let her catch up. The scientists came stumbling out of their tents as I passed, demanding to know what was happening.

'The hole!' I shouted, not slowing down. 'Someone's been hurt at the hole!'

I ran on, leaving everyone else behind. It was obvious now that I'd been lured away by the movements in the dark. Decoyed to the part of the site furthest from the hole. And while I stood there, like an idiot, staring out into the dark, someone or something had moved quietly round the perimeter to its true target. The hole.

When I finally got there, Robert was lying sprawled on the ground, not moving. His left arm was gone, severed neatly at the shoulder. No blood pumped from the wound, not even a drop, and there was no sign of the arm itself anywhere. No blood on the grass beside the hole. Penny finally caught up with me, and then clutched my arm with both hands as she saw the body. Paul, Mike and Ellie stumbled to a halt beside us. The Professor was the last to arrive, breathing hard.

Ellie didn't scream or cry when she saw what had happened to Robert. All the colour drained out of her face, and she made a sound that was as much a moan as anything else. Mike took her quietly by the shoulders and turned her away, to stop her staring at the body. She buried her face in his shoulder. He held her tightly, not looking at Robert. Paul looked from the body to the hole and then back again; as though he felt he should be doing something, but didn't know what. The Professor looked at Robert for a long moment, her mouth working as she tried to decide what to say.

'His arm must have been cut off by the hole's edge,' she said finally. 'That's the only thing that could have made a cut as clean as that. Perhaps he stumbled and stretched out his arm to stop himself falling . . . But what was he doing? I told everyone to stay behind the line!'

'The hole took his arm the same way it took the end of the branch you showed me earlier,' I said.

'Why are the hole's edges so incredibly sharp?' said Penny, perhaps just to be asking something.

'The hole isn't part of our reality,' said Paul. 'It was punched through from somewhere else. The edge is where two different sets of rules meet and argue it out as to which of them is in charge.'

'Why isn't there any blood?' said Penny.

'The hole creates its own gravity, close up,' said the Professor. 'It would have sucked all the blood in. Along with the arm.'

'Stop it!' said Ellie, her face still buried in Mike's shoulder. 'Please, just stop being so . . . reasonable!'

'We need to understand what's happened, Ellie,' said Mike.

'We know what's happened,' said Ellie. 'Robert's dead. The hole killed him.'

'But if he fell against the edge and the hole took his arm off,' said Penny, 'why didn't all of him go in?'

'That's the question you're going with?' said Mike. 'Really? Not what was he doing out here on his own? Or why he crossed the line? There's only one answer that makes any sense. Someone must have pushed him in.'

'Who would do that?' said Ellie, raising her head from Mike's shoulder.

A woman who was tired of him, I thought, but didn't say.

'Who would benefit from his death?' said the Professor, looking at Mike.

'I just got here,' Mike said steadily. 'You all saw me, just as I saw you. This is nothing to do with me.'

'Robert had more sense than to go anywhere near the hole,' said Ellie. 'Someone must have done this to him.'

'Why did he leave your tent?' I said.

'He couldn't sleep. Neither could I. Then we thought we heard something moving around behind our tent.' Ellie shook her head slowly. 'He said he was going outside to take a look. I didn't ask him to! I told him not to. He said he'd only be a minute. He just needed to make sure it was nothing, check it out for our peace of mind. He left the tent and I sat there, waiting for him to come back and tell me it was nothing. So we could laugh, and get some sleep at last. But he didn't come back. And then . . . I heard him scream.'

'We all heard him scream,' said Mike.

'You all came out of your tents fast enough,' I said.

'I don't think any of us were sleeping,' said Paul.

'Did the rest of you hear movements in the night?' I said. 'Did you hear Robert leave his tent? Or anyone else leave theirs?'

They all looked at each other. None of them appeared certain about anything. It seemed likely that, despite their protestations, they'd all been at least half-asleep. In the time it had taken them to get out of their sleeping bags and out of their tents, any one of them could have made their way back from the hole.

'You were on guard!' the Professor said angrily to me. 'Didn't you see anything?'

'Penny and I were decoyed to the other side of the camp,' I said.

'Could something have come out of the hole and attacked Robert?' said Mike.

'More likely it was somebody,' said the Professor.

'You mean one of us?' said Ellie.

The three scientists stared at the Professor, but she wouldn't back down.

'You were all thinking it,' she said flatly. 'It has to be more likely that it was one of you than some unknown alien or a legendary Beast. Any of you could have left your tent quietly, and the others wouldn't have known anything about it.'

'Including you,' said Mike.

She didn't quite laugh in his face. 'You really think a woman my age could overcome someone Robert's size?'

'You wouldn't need to,' said Mike. 'He wouldn't have seen you as a threat. All you had to do was get behind him and push.'

'Stop it!' said Ellie. 'Please, Mike, you're not helping.'

'Robert heard something,' the Professor said doggedly.

'Something that lured him out of his tent, and all the way over to the hole. And while he was concentrating on that, he could have been caught off guard by anyone.'

'But what if something did come out of the hole?' Paul said slowly. 'Some unknown thing that tried to take him. And he struggled and the attacker settled for just an arm?'

'How can you talk like that, with Robert lying dead at our feet?' said Ellie, her voice rising.

'We're scientists,' the Professor said steadily. 'We have to look at the evidence before us calmly and objectively.'

'You heartless cow!' said Ellie.

'Hush, Ellie, hush,' said Mike.

She broke away from him. He started to reach out to her, but she wouldn't even look at him. He shrugged uncertainly.

'We're just trying to figure out what happened, Ellie. It's what we do.'

They were all doing their best to be calm and scientific, but none of them were used to sudden death and the cold realities of bodies. It probably helped a little that the dark hole and the flat fierce light made the scene seem almost unreal.

'I told you we should have barricaded the hole,' said Ellie.

'It wouldn't have stopped an invader,' said Paul.

'You really think that's what happened here?' said Mike.

'Don't you?' said Ellie.

The Professor made a flat, disgusted sound. 'You want it to be an alien predator, because that has to be preferable to the idea that one of us is a cold-blooded killer.'

Ellie turned abruptly to glare at me. 'How could you let this happen? You were supposed to be on guard!'

'We heard movements, too,' I said. 'We were lured away, just so this could happen.'

'What kind of movements?' said Mike.

'Something large and heavy, circling the camp in the dark,' said Penny. 'Might have been human, might not.'

'If it was out there in the dark, how could it see?' said Paul.

'We were in the light,' I said. 'And after that, all it had to do was follow the perimeter to the hole.'

'Could it have been the Beast?' said Ellie.

She desperately wanted me to say 'No, of course not!', but

I couldn't say that. She shook her head, disappointed, and turned away. We all stared out at the heavy night surrounding the camp's pitifully small circle of light. The night stared back at us, silent and menacing. A darkness so absolute it could hide anything. Anything at all.

'I think we need to leave right now,' said Mike.

'Leave?' said the Professor. 'And give up on the greatest scientific find of our time? Over what could be just another stupid accident? Get a grip on yourself, Mike!'

'The hole isn't worth dying over!' said Mike.

'We're not in any danger, as long as we keep our heads,' said the Professor.

'And how likely is that, given that Robert's just lost his arm?'

'Mike, please!' said Ellie.

'Robert's death was no accident,' said Paul. 'He had more sense.'

'Exactly,' said Mike. 'Which means we're all in danger. I say we get the hell out of here while we still can.'

'If you leave, you know what to expect,' the Professor said coldly. 'You can forget all those generous research grants, and you can be sure the Government will find some way to punish you for running out on them.'

Mike hesitated, and then he looked at Ellie and his resolve settled. 'I'm going, and Ellie's going with me. Anyone else want to do the sane and sensible thing?'

'Hold it!' I said. 'The only transport we have is Penny's car, and that's parked some way down the hill. You really want to leave the light and go stumbling off through the dark? How far do you think you'll get if what we heard is still out there?'

Everyone looked at the darkness. Nobody moved.

'We're safer here, together,' I said steadily. 'Whatever's going on. Let's go back to the fire, where we can keep an eye on each other. I'll put Robert's body in with Terry. Then we just stick together until the night is over, and request reinforcements and protection from Mr Carroll when he makes his call.'

Mike looked at Ellie. 'Is that what you want?'

She nodded silently. The others were nodding too. Penny moved in close beside me, and lowered her voice.

'You still have your phone, Ishmael. You could call the Colonel right now. Have him send people in to secure the site and get the scientists out of here.'

'I already thought of that,' I said quietly. 'I didn't mention it because if one of these people is a murderer, I don't want to risk them scattering once they're away from here. And if there is some alien predator out there in the dark, I don't want to risk offering it more targets of opportunity.'

'They're muttering again . . .' said Mike.

'Not now, Mike!' said Ellie.

I looked at the Professor. 'It's your team. The Colonel put you in charge. What do you say?'

She looked at the hole. 'If we leave, they'll take this opportunity away from us. You know they will. I say we stay by the fire and wait for Mr Carroll's call. We should be perfectly safe as long as we stay in the light.'

She set off down the hill. The others followed after her. I looked at Penny.

'You know this is the only sensible thing to do.'

'As long as we can keep them alive till morning,' she said.

THREE
Something's Watching

We sat round the fire, the scientists staring out into the night like cavemen fearful of the dark and all the unknown horrors it might hold. The entire campsite was bathed in a fierce glow from the perimeter lights, but the darkness outside had a force and power all its own. I'd made sure everyone was spread out around the fire. So we could be sure of seeing in every direction at once, so nothing could sneak up on us. I didn't need to tell them. After a while, Mike picked up a handful of branches from the pile beside the fire.

'The fire's fine,' I said. 'Leave it be.'

'The bigger the better, as far as I'm concerned,' said Mike, finding some comfort in his usual role of always being up for an argument. 'It's getting pretty damned cold out here on the side of this hill, in case you hadn't noticed. And what makes you such an expert on everything, anyway? You're not even that great a security man, with two of us dead on your watch.'

'Both of whom might still be alive if they'd listened to me,' I said steadily. 'We have to be careful with our supply of fuel. Because that's all we've got to keep the fire going until the sun comes up and we can safely go out to look for more firewood. Unless you feel like wandering around in the dark on your own?'

'No, he doesn't,' said Ellie. She gave Mike a stern look, and he dropped the branches back on the pile and looked away. Ellie managed a small smile for the rest of us. 'He always feels the need to fix something when he can't put right what really needs fixing.'

'I'm sorry about Robert,' I said. 'And Terry. But there was nothing I could do for either of them.'

'I know that,' said Ellie.

'How are you feeling, Ellie?' said Mike.

She shrugged. 'I feel . . . strange. I should be collapsing in a flood of tears, but that's never been me. I just feel numb . . . like I've had my life kicked out of me. I thought I knew what I was doing, and where I was going. And now Robert is dead, and I don't know anything.'

Paul leaned forward and fixed me with a steady gaze across the fire. 'Who do you think killed Robert? Or should that be *what* killed him?'

'I still say it was most likely an accident,' the Professor said stubbornly, not looking at any of us.

'Oh, come on!' said Mike, unable to stay quiet any longer. 'Terry *and* Robert? Both of them dead because of the hole? Let's try to act like adults and bite the bullet. Terry and Robert were murdered. And since there's no one else here, the murderer has to be one of us.'

'No it doesn't,' said Ellie. 'There has to be some other explanation.'

'I don't believe in legendary Beasts,' Mike said flatly. 'Or some hypothetical alien sneaking in and out of the hole when no one's looking. I also don't believe in foreign superspies creeping into camp to steal our secrets. Especially since we haven't come up with anything worth stealing. So that just leaves us. A small group of people who barely know each other, brought together by outside forces. We haven't been here twenty-four hours and already two of us are dead! You still want to talk about accidents?'

'Let's not forget the archaeologist,' said Paul.

'Yes,' said Mike, 'that makes three deaths connected with the hole!'

'The hole is dangerous,' said the Professor. 'That's why we put down the safety line. The archaeologist tripped and fell in. Terry decided to ignore all our safety protocols and jumped in. Robert . . . shouldn't have been there on his own, and he definitely should have known better than to get that close.'

'There's none so blind as those who stick their fingers in their eyes,' said Mike. 'Three deaths is more than coincidence. It's enemy action.'

'So who are you accusing?' said Ellie.

There was a long pause, as everyone looked at everyone else and no one said anything. Because the idea was just too unfamiliar for the Professor and her team to cope with. They could handle theoretical physics and dimensional doorways, but the concept of cold-blooded murder was way outside their experience. Penny looked at me, but I didn't say anything either. Because I had no clues, no clear motives, and no theories that made any sense. In the end, Mike looked at me challengingly.

'You're the security man. What do you think?'

'I don't see any evidence that points to anyone in particular,' I said carefully. 'Or any reason why any of you would want to kill Terry or Robert. Unless you think I'm missing something?'

'Everything was fine until you turned up,' said Paul.

He didn't put any emphasis in his voice. Just left the statement lying there for everyone to consider.

'We were summoned here, just like you,' I said.

'And we were together when Robert died,' said Penny. 'On the other side of the camp, far away from the hole.'

'Well, you would say that, wouldn't you?' said Mike.

'Why would we want to kill two people we never met before today?' I said, careful to keep my voice calm and reasonable.

'How do we know you didn't?' Mike said cunningly. 'We don't know anything about you.'

'Ishmael and Penny are supposed to be here,' the Professor said firmly. 'The Colonel told me to expect them, and vouched for both of them personally.'

'Hold it!' said Mike. 'He might have told you to expect an Ishmael Jones and a Penny Belcourt, but how do we know this is them? The real them? Just because they say so? Did they show you any official ID when they arrived?'

'People like us don't carry official identification,' I said. 'We're not that kind of security.'

'How very convenient!' said Mike.

'They could be the foreign spies,' said Ellie, sitting up straight. 'Here to steal what we've discovered about the hole.'

'But you haven't found out anything yet,' said Penny.

'You didn't know that before you got here,' Ellie said sharply. 'Maybe Robert saw something or heard something that made him suspicious of you, so you had to kill him to shut him up.'

'Exactly!' said Mike. 'All you had to do was sneak up behind him and push him against the edge of the hole.'

'I suggest you wait till the eight a.m. call,' I said, 'and describe us to Mr Carroll. He can identify us. Or ask the Colonel for a code phrase so you can be sure we are who we say we are. But the real proof that we are the real security people is that Penny and I could have killed you all in your tents, when you were at your most vulnerable and most off guard. The very fact that you're all still alive speaks against your argument. Because if we wanted you dead, you'd be dead.'

'Not exactly the most reassuring way to prove our bona fides, darling!' murmured Penny.

But the scientists thought it through and finally nodded reluctantly. Ellie slumped tiredly, as the energy from her argument subsided.

'I still don't see why anyone would want to kill Robert,' she said quietly. 'It doesn't make any sense.'

'Perhaps someone wanted his woman,' said Paul.

Mike sat up straight, glaring at him. 'Are you accusing me?'

'Where were you, Mike?' said Paul, meeting his gaze steadily. 'What were you doing when Robert was killed?'

'I was in my tent,' said Mike.

'Alone,' said the Professor. 'With no alibi.'

'Yes,' said Mike, 'just like the rest of you!'

'The rest of us weren't jealous of Robert,' said Paul.

'Penny and I were on guard,' I said, cutting the argument short before it could get out of hand. 'I didn't hear Robert leave his tent or spot him sneaking past us to get to the hole, which means he must have been really quiet. So I have to ask, what reason could he have for not wanting to be noticed? What might he have been intending to do at the hole that he wouldn't want anyone else to know about?'

Mike looked at me curiously. 'Is your hearing really so good that you would hear him tiptoeing past you on grass?'

'Yes,' I said. 'It comes with the job. Before I came here, I would have bet good money no one could sneak past me without my noticing. But it seems to me that none of my senses are as sharp as they should be. I think the hole is having an effect on all of us. Do the rest of you feel as sharp as usual?'

They all thought about that, and then frowned. Not liking the implications of where their thoughts were going.

'That could explain why our work hasn't been going anywhere,' the Professor said finally.

'Oh, come on!' said Mike. 'It's our first day.'

'But you're all supposed to be geniuses,' the Professor said coldly. 'The best in your fields, and cutting-edge theorists. That's why I put your names on the list.'

'She's right,' said Ellie. 'We should have come up with something by now.'

'I think we want one of us to be the murderer,' Paul said flatly, 'rather than face the possibility that something from inside the hole is responsible. But is that because the idea is just too much for us? Or because the hole doesn't want us to think that? If the hole is interfering with our thoughts, how can we be sure anything we come up with is our own idea? The only way to be certain is to obtain some direct observations of what's going on inside the hole. We need to see it for ourselves.'

'No, Paul,' the Professor said immediately. 'No one else is going into the hole, under any circumstances. Not after what happened to Terry.'

'Really?' said Mike. 'What did happen to Terry?'

'Does it matter?' said Ellie. 'You saw his face!'

'We need to know what's going on inside the hole!' said Paul. 'Before whatever's in there comes out to kill again.'

'I don't believe there's anything in there,' Mike said doggedly. 'Or that the hole is somehow messing with our heads.'

'That's probably because the hole *is* messing with your head,' said Paul.

'So,' I said, 'any volunteers to strap the cable to their back and do what Terry did? Even after you saw the look on his face?'

I looked around the fire, but they were all avoiding each other's eyes. And yet, even though none of them felt like putting themselves forward, it was clear they weren't ready to give up on the idea.

'Do you have any breathing apparatus?' Penny said suddenly. 'Or some kind of survival suit? Terry went into the hole entirely unprotected, like a deep-sea diver jumping in without any scuba gear. That could be why he didn't survive.'

'We don't need anything like that,' Paul said flatly. 'One of the first things I did was to lower some of my test animals a few feet into the hole and then bring them out again, before I tried sending them down any distance. They all emerged completely unaffected.'

'How can you be sure?' said Mike, just to be contentious. 'They couldn't tell you what it was like in there.'

'I examined them all carefully,' said Paul. 'No change in any of their life signs, no radiation or chemical residues, nothing to indicate they'd suffered any harm. And they didn't seem in the least disturbed by the experience. Simple exposure to what's inside the hole is not immediately fatal. Terry knew that. That's why he was so ready to go in himself.'

'Still, Terry's dead,' said Ellie.

'But we don't know why,' said Paul. 'There was no obvious cause of death.'

'It was shock,' said Mike. 'He saw something in there, and just seeing it was enough to kill him. Something too horrible for the human mind to bear.'

'Then none of us should go in,' said Ellie.

'But a security man with experience of death and dangerous places might fare better than a sheltered young scientist,' said the Professor.

They all looked at me, and I could see they liked the idea. I wasn't one of them, and I was the one who'd been sent to keep them safe but had let two of them die. I thought about it. Perhaps I did have a responsibility to go in, because I was the only one who might be able to look the Medusa in the eye and live to tell of it. Penny saw the way my thoughts were going and put a hand on my arm, her fingers clamping down hard.

'You are *not* going in there, Ishmael. The only sure way to keep everyone safe is to find the murderer. To discover who or what is killing these people. And you can't do that by putting yourself in danger. You can't go, you're needed here.'

'But I am the most likely to survive a trip into the hole,' I said. 'Because of my background.'

Which was as close as I could come in public to reminding Penny I was more than human in some ways.

'The hole needs a scientist,' Penny said determinedly, 'to make sense of what's in there.'

'Not necessarily,' said Mike, smiling unpleasantly. 'We just need to know whether there's a Beast at the bottom of the hole.'

'All right,' said Penny. 'How about this? What if this whole argument is just an excuse devised by someone to get rid of the only person here with experience of identifying murderers?'

They all stopped and looked at each other sharply. The thought hadn't occurred to them.

'That makes sense,' I said. 'So I think I'll politely decline the honour of taking a giant leap into the dark for all mankind. I've got a better idea. Rather than risking one of us, why not just lower in a camera?'

'Because that was practically the first thing we tried when we got here,' said Paul. 'I put a video camera in. And when that didn't work, I tried a stills camera. But something in the hole doesn't want its photo taken.'

'The cameras didn't work?' said Penny.

'No way of knowing,' said Paul. 'None of them came back.'

'We sent in half a dozen different cameras,' said the Professor. 'Initially on their own, and then inside secure specimen cages. But every time we pulled the cable back out, the camera was gone.'

'But we didn't try a live broadcast,' said Ellie.

'There's no guarantee the camera's signal would reach us from inside the hole,' said Paul. 'And anyway, Black Heir didn't think to supply us with that kind of camera. Bit of an oversight, really.'

'Mike brought one with him,' said Ellie.

We all looked at Mike, who was looking at Ellie as though she'd betrayed a confidence.

'Why didn't you tell us, Mike?' demanded the Professor. 'And what are you doing with such a thing anyway? I was told there wasn't enough time to pack any personal belongings.'

'It was in my pocket,' said Mike. 'Because I was getting ready to go on holiday when I was bustled away. And I didn't say anything because it's *my* camera . . . and it was very expensive!'

'Whatever he's got, it's bound to be top of the line, with all kinds of extra bells and whistles,' said Ellie. 'Mike always has to have the best toys.'

'Sounds like just the thing,' I said.

Everyone looked at Mike. He tried to stand on his dignity and stare us all down, but that didn't last long.

'Oh, all right!' he said, scowling ungraciously. 'It's in my tent. I'll go and get it. But you'd better treat it carefully!'

Ellie went with him to his tent. Partly to keep him company and partly to show she was sorry for speaking up. Mike let her. They came back with the camera, and Mike handed it over to Paul.

'You're always saying you're the tech wizard here. Will this do the job?'

Paul studied the camera carefully, then strode up the hill to the equipment centre to check the camera was compatible with his computer. The rest of us trailed after him. The scientists looked glad to be doing something at last. Paul fired up his monitor screen, and Mike hovered at Paul's shoulder while he worked, not unlike an anxious parent. Paul made a few adjustments and then nodded, satisfied.

'Ready to go.'

'Are you sure you know how to work it properly?' said Mike, who seemed almost on the edge of snatching his camera back. 'I mean, it has all kind of settings . . .'

'Actually,' said Paul, 'this is pretty standard. If you really paid top rate, they saw you coming. But it's perfectly suitable for our needs.' He stopped and looked at Mike. 'Why did you feel the need for a live-broadcast camera on holiday?'

'Some of us have a life outside science,' said Mike.

'Don't press him,' said Ellie. 'Trust me, it's not going to be anything you want to know about.'

'We'll need a specimen cage to put the camera in,' said Paul. 'The protection might buy us enough time for a good look round.'

He went to get one. Mike started to go with him. And then stopped, not wanting to leave Ellie. She made a point of not noticing.

'Did the other camera cages get smashed when they were lowered into the hole?' said Penny.

'No,' said the Professor. 'Something smashed the lock, removed the camera, and left the empty cage still attached for us to find when we pulled it back out.'

I looked at her. 'But that implies a conscious mind, making decisions. Proof that there is something in the hole.'

'Not necessarily,' said the Professor, not giving an inch. 'Without knowing what conditions are like inside the hole, we can't be sure of anything.'

Paul came back with a suitably sturdy cage, placed the camera inside, and locked the front panel. While he was doing that, the Professor went over to the steel drum and started up the engine. She got the cable moving, and brought the end over to the equipment centre. Paul attached the clasp to the back of the cage; and then rattled it hard a few times, just to make sure it was secure.

'Ready,' he said. 'The camera is running, and according to my monitor we have a strong signal.'

'Give it to me,' I said. 'I'll drop it into the hole.'

'Wait for the monitor to grab on to the signal,' he said. He thrust the camera cage into Mike's hands and bent over before the screen, his hands moving quickly across the keyboard. 'Wait for it, wait for it . . . Yes, there it is.'

Mike panned the camera back and forth. The rest of us crowded before the monitor, watching an image of us watching ourselves on the screen. I turned to Mike and put out a hand for the camera, but he shook his head firmly.

'It's my camera. If anyone's going to throw it into the hole, I should be the one to do it.'

'He always was funny about who got to handle his equipment,' said Ellie, to no one in particular.

We all pretended we hadn't heard that. Apart from Mike,

who gave Ellie a disbelieving look. She gave him a surprisingly demure smile in return. People get over shock in the strangest ways. I cleared my throat, in a reminding sort of way, and headed for the hole. Mike went with me. We approached the hole cautiously, treating it like a wild animal that might lash out at us, given a chance. The steel cable unwound steadily behind us. I made sure we stopped well short of the safety line, and Mike aimed his camera at the hole.

'What are you seeing?' I called back.

'Just a black circle,' Paul said loudly. 'Flat, featureless, no depth or details. At least the camera can see the hole . . . Which proves something, I suppose.'

Mike took one careful step over the safety line, and extended the cage towards the hole. I stood ready to grab hold of him and haul him back, if necessary. Mike lightly tossed the cage towards the hole, and the surface gravity grabbed hold of it and pulled it in. The camera disappeared into the darkness as though into a pool of black water, without leaving even the slightest ripple on the surface. Mike stepped quickly back behind the line, waited a moment to be sure the cable was disappearing into the hole after the cage, and then turned and hurried back down the hill to join the others standing in front of the monitor. I stayed where I was, studying the hole, ready for any reaction. But there wasn't one. The hole seemed entirely indifferent to whatever we did. I turned my back on it, and went back down the hill to the equipment centre.

The cable descended steadily into the hole, lowering the camera into the darkness. Everyone crammed together before the monitor, intent on the screen. I had to shoulder a few people aside to get to the front, but no one objected. Not after they saw the look on my face. For quite a while nothing showed on the screen, not even static. The Professor stirred unhappily, and turned to Paul.

'Are you sure this thing is working?'

Paul shrugged helplessly. 'The image cut off the moment the camera went into the hole. The signal is still strong, but we're not getting a picture.'

'What about sound?' said Penny, pressing against my back

as she peered over my shoulder. 'Mike, can your camera pick up sound?'

'Of course!' he said, outraged at the very idea he'd spend good money on a camera that couldn't.

'There's nothing to suggest anything inside the hole is interfering with the signal,' said Paul.

'Maybe we're only seeing darkness because that's all there is inside the hole,' said Ellie.

'Then what did Terry see?' said the Professor.

An interesting question. To which no one had an answer.

We watched the empty screen, straining our eyes against a darkness that gave nothing away. The only sound in the camp was the steady unwinding of cable from the drum, and the slow hum of its engine. And then suddenly a light appeared, right in the middle of the screen. We all leaned forward.

'What is that?' I said.

'I don't know,' said Paul. 'As far as my readings can tell, it's just . . . light. Still, this is a first. Proof there is something on the other side of the hole apart from darkness.'

'But are we looking at a small light close to the camera, or a much bigger light further away?' said Penny.

'Now that is a good question,' said Paul. 'Unfortunately, I have absolutely no way of telling.'

'I suppose it could be the light at the end of the tunnel . . .' said Mike.

'I told you the hole was a connection between this world and somewhere else!' said Ellie. 'We could be looking at light from another planet.'

'Is there any way to zoom in on the light?' asked the Professor.

'Mike's camera is actually pretty basic,' said Paul. 'No zoom, no ultraviolet or infrared . . .'

'Why would I want any of that on holiday?' said Mike.

'Why would you want to broadcast your holiday live?' said Paul.

'Mike has always been very visually orientated,' Ellie said demurely.

'You're punishing me for something, aren't you, Ellie?' said Mike.

'Can we tell how far the camera has descended?' I asked, at least partly in self-defence.

Paul worked his keyboard again, and a number appeared in the bottom right-hand corner of the screen, steadily increasing.

'That's how much cable has been played out so far,' he said. 'Forty-seven feet, fifty feet . . . Still descending into the dark. The light doesn't seem to be getting any closer, or any brighter.'

'How much cable is there on the drum?' asked Penny.

'Three hundred feet,' said the Professor. 'I suppose Black Heir didn't expect us to need any more than that.'

We kept watching as the camera fell further and further away from us. The light didn't change in size or intensity. We passed a hundred feet, and then a hundred and fifty. A slow chill passed through me, as I thought about the camera disappearing down a deep shaft that had nothing at all to do with the interior of the hill.

'What happens if we get to the end of the cable and we still haven't reached the light?' said Penny.

'Then we'll have to pull the camera back up and think of something else,' I said. 'Hopefully the recording will tell us something about the hole's interior. You are recording this, Paul?'

'No, I'm a complete amateur who's never worked with communications equipment before,' said Paul, not looking round. 'Of course I'm recording!'

'We could just leave the camera dangling there,' said Ellie. 'Like bait. See if something shows up to grab it.'

'But it's my camera!' said Mike.

'Maybe Black Heir will recompense you,' said Ellie.

Mike sniffed loudly. 'Yeah, that'll happen.'

'Hush!' said the Professor.

'At least this camera is still there,' I said. 'All the other cameras you sent down were taken. So what's different, this time?'

'This one's sending a signal out of the hole,' said Paul. 'But maybe what's in there doesn't want to approach the camera, for fear of being seen.'

'What reason could it have to be scared of us?' said Penny.

'Perhaps it thinks that if we don't know what it is, we won't be able to defend ourselves properly against it,' I said.

'We just passed two hundred feet,' said Paul, 'and still nothing's happening. Maybe it's just not there anymore.'

'Or maybe it thinks three deaths are enough,' said the Professor. 'That it's had enough tribute.'

I looked at the Professor. 'You really think that's what's happening here?'

'I don't know what to think,' she said, not taking her eyes off the screen.

Suddenly, there was a sound. Faint at first, just a murmur in the distance. We all leaned forward automatically, but getting closer to the screen didn't help. It wasn't any kind of voice; it was too regular for that. The sound quickly grew louder, developing into a slow, steady thudding, heavy enough to make all of us wince.

'What is that?' said Mike.

'It sounds like a heartbeat,' I said. 'From something really big.'

'Why do you never have anything good to tell us?' said Mike.

'Hold it! The sound isn't coming from the monitor's speakers!' said Paul. He had to raise his voice to make himself heard. 'That means the sound isn't part of the camera's signal.'

'If it's not coming from inside the hole,' I said, 'that means it has to be out here, with us.'

We all looked around quickly, but there was nothing moving in the camp. Nothing that could be responsible for such a noise. And yet it sounded as though the source was somewhere close at hand, definitely not in the darkness outside the camp. The scientists scattered to check out their various pieces of equipment, but the sound wasn't coming from any of them. None of their instruments could tell what the sound was, or where it was coming from. I closed my eyes so I could concentrate, but no matter which way I turned my head I couldn't pin the sound down. It was just there, in the equipment centre with us. As though we weren't alone any more. I opened my eyes as the scientists returned to crowd before the monitor again. The sound was now so loud it was almost overwhelming, like the heartbeat of some impossibly huge thing, hammering on the air. I was surprised the whole equipment centre wasn't shaking and shuddering from the strength of it.

'Is the sound getting louder or closer?' said Penny. She had to shout to make herself heard. 'Is it coming our way from somewhere else?'

'It could be coming up out of the hole,' Ellie shouted back. 'I think we should get out of here!'

'Where could we go?' the Professor said loudly.

Mike put a comforting arm around Ellie, and she let him do it.

I looked up the hill towards the hole, but the flat black surface just stared back at me like a disinterested unblinking eye. I looked around the camp, but it was still empty. If there was something there, I couldn't see it. Perhaps . . . it was just too alien, too other, to be seen. The sound grew painfully loud, an assault on the senses. Ellie clapped her hands over her ears. We all flinched at every heartbeat, as if trying to get away from it. I could feel the sound vibrating in my bones. And then it stopped. The sudden silence was a blessing, and we all breathed heavy sighs of relief. As though a real but unknown danger had passed us by. Ellie slowly took her hands away from her ears, but she didn't lower them, as if half-expecting the sounds to start up again at any moment. And then Paul stabbed a finger at the monitor screen.

'We've got something!'

Sharp flashes of light flared out of the screen, blasting into our faces. The others had to turn their heads away, blinded by the light, but I kept watching. There was something in the light . . . Something I thought I almost understood. The intensity of the light died down, but the flashes continued: a series of images that came and went too quickly to grasp. I leaned forward, frowning into the light as I concentrated, but it was hard to get more than a basic impression of what I was looking at. The others turned their faces back to the screen, and then pressed forward, intrigued, until we were all right on top of the monitor screen. The images appeared and disappeared unsettlingly quickly, almost subliminal. I got a feeling of artificial structures the size of mountains . . . A night sky that

opened up like a gigantic eye . . . A rain of dying stars . . . I
wasn't sure whether any of it was real, or whether what I was
seeing was just my mind struggling to interpret the images.

'I'm not seeing anything clearly,' said Penny. 'But it's
making me feel bad. As though I shouldn't be looking at
things like this.'

There was a general murmur of agreement from the
scientists.

'There's something almost disturbing about what we're
being shown . . .' said Mike.

'It has to be some form of communication,' said Paul.

'Then why are they making it so difficult for us?' said Mike.

'Maybe this is the best they can do,' said Paul. 'We might
not have even basic concepts in common, such as scales of
reference or linear time.'

'I feel like I should be watching through my fingers,' said
Ellie. 'Like when I was a teenager, watching old horror movies
late at night.'

'Concentrate!' the Professor said harshly. 'This is our first
communication from inside the hole. It has to mean something.
Why is the hole showing us this?'

'Why is it blasting the back of my head off with this stuff?'
said Mike.

'Maybe it has to do it this way,' said Paul. 'Because our
minds could only cope with what it has to show in short
glimpses. Maybe it learned to hold back after what happened
to Terry.'

'It feels like we're watching individual frames of a film,'
said Ellie. 'One still at a time. Because if we saw the whole
moving picture and understood it, it would destroy our minds.
Like Terry.'

Penny shot me a look, but all I could do was shake my
head. I had no extra insights to offer. Except . . . I couldn't
shake the feeling that Ellie was right. That we shouldn't be
looking at any of this, because it was dangerous.

The images shut off abruptly, and we all made varying
sounds of relief. The others shook their heads and rubbed their
eyes, like that would help. But no one turned away from the
monitor.

'Did anyone get anything specific from that?' I said.

'Just a real pig of a headache,' said Mike.

'I don't think any of it came through the camera,' said Paul. 'It's more like something else piggybacked the signal to get to us.'

'How does everyone feel?' asked the Professor. 'Answer me, people! I'm not just talking because I like the sound of my own voice.'

'Could have fooled me,' muttered Mike.

'I feel like I just woke up from a nightmare I can't remember,' said Ellie. 'I kept wanting to look away from the screen, but I couldn't.'

'It was fascinating,' said Paul. 'In a horrible sort of way.'

'No,' said Ellie. 'I mean, whatever was showing us those images wouldn't let us look away. Not until it was finished with us.'

'You're right,' said Mike. 'That didn't feel like communication. It was more like brainwashing.'

'Let's not spook ourselves,' the Professor said sternly. 'It's just information provided in an unfamiliar way. It's up to us to interpret it.'

'Whatever it is that's in the hole took over the live broadcast as a way to get to us,' said Paul.

'Whatever it was saying, it didn't feel at all friendly,' said Ellie.

'Maybe it was saying "Stay out of my yard!"?' said Mike.

'Hold it!' said Paul. 'Something's happening.'

A new image had appeared, filling the monitor screen. It took me a moment to realize we were looking at a distorted view of ourselves standing before the screen. As though something was looking over our shoulders. I looked behind us, but there was nothing there. I turned back to the screen. In the view we were being shown, we appeared strange, misshapen, alien. The light surrounding us wasn't the flat fierce glare of the perimeter lights; on the screen it was a harsh reddish orange, foul and unhealthy, like light that had soured and gone off. The figures crouching before the screen looked twisted and monstrous; everything about their shapes and dimensions was hideously wrong. The equipment scattered around the centre looked like a mad tangle of things that made no sense. There was a general feeling of disgust and disquiet to the image on the screen. As though we were looking at things that shouldn't exist.

'It feels . . . like when I see a spider scuttling towards me,' said Penny, 'and all I want to do is stamp on it before it can get to me.'

'Arachnid revulsion . . .' said Mike.

'What *is* this?' said the Professor. 'Where is it coming from?'

'This time the signal is definitely coming from the camera,' said Paul.

'It can't be!' said Mike. 'The camera's in the hole. This is a view from behind us.'

'Why do we look like that?' said Penny.

'I think this is how whatever is in the hole sees us,' I said. 'As monsters, aliens, abominations. We're being sent a message, and not a good one. If you see something as a monster, that allows you to attack it.'

'Like the spider,' said Penny. 'Even though it probably doesn't mean any harm.'

'What if this is how it sees itself?' said the Professor. 'Interpreting us according to its own lights?'

'But that's not how it feels,' I said, 'is it?'

'No,' said Ellie. 'It feels like a slap in the face.'

'Rage, disgust, horror . . .' said Mike.

'Humanity seen through the eyes of a Beast,' said Paul.

The screen went blank.

'What's happened?' said the Professor. 'Paul, get the image back!'

Paul worked quickly at his keyboard, then shook his head. 'There's no feed from the camera. It's shut down.'

'Have you broken my camera?' said Mike.

'Can't you restart the broadcast from here?' said Ellie.

'There's no signal at all,' said Paul. 'Either the camera is broken, or something's taken it.'

'You've lost my camera!' said Mike. 'I knew it . . .'

'Shut up, Mike!' said Ellie. 'Let me think . . . If the camera had simply been snatched off the end of the cable, it would still be broadcasting.'

'Maybe it's been shut down because whatever's in the hole has nothing more to say to us,' I said.

'Bring the cable back up,' said the Professor.

Paul hurried out of the equipment centre and headed for the steel drum. He threw on the brake, waited for the cable to come to a halt, and then put the engine into reverse. The cable thrummed and quivered as it came back up out of the hole, and we all watched silently as it emerged from the black surface, foot by foot. It appeared entirely unaffected by its time in the hole. I kept glancing at the monitor, but it remained completely blank. The cable wound itself steadily back on to the drum, without any sudden jerks or interruptions. There was a growing tension in the equipment centre, a feeling of uneasy anticipation. I braced myself, just in case something had grabbed hold of the end of the cable and was riding it, up out of the dark. I was ready to run up to the hole, knock it loose, and kick it back in without a moment's hesitation. Because after everything I'd seen, I wasn't ready to let anything from the hole into this world.

When the last of the cable jumped out of the hole and bumped across the grass, the specimen cage was still attached. The moment it appeared, Paul shut down the drum's engine and hurried back to join us. We all left the equipment centre and hurried up the hill to stand over the cage as it lay on the ground. The front panel was hanging open, and the camera was gone.

'I knew it!' said Mike.

'Why didn't it just grab the cage?' said Penny.

'It wanted to show us what it can do,' said Paul.

'Maybe it thinks it can learn about us by studying the things we send into the hole,' said Ellie.

'Given everything it just showed us,' I said, 'I think we have to assume it isn't friendly. Perhaps it thought the camera was getting too close, and sent us those images to prevent us from seeing what the camera was seeing. Because it doesn't want us to know what it is.'

'But why would it feel that way?' said Penny. 'I mean, why would it care? Why would it feel the need to hide anything from us?'

'Terry saw it,' said Ellie. 'Something too horrible for the human mind to bear.'

'Man was never meant to look on the Medusa,' said the Professor. 'I don't think whatever's in the hole gives a damn about us. It just doesn't want us to know anything about it.'

'Then why send the hole here in the first place?' said Penny. 'Why establish a tunnel or spy hole into another world, if you're only going to have a fit of the vapours the first time you see something different from you?'

'You don't have to like the inhabitants to want to take their world,' said Ellie. 'I told you, this is an invasion point. We have to block off the hole.'

'Give me time,' I said. 'I'll think of something. We're not in any immediate danger; whatever's in there is not going to take us by surprise. There are more lights covering the hole than there are everywhere else.' Then I stopped, and looked around me. 'As long as the lights stay on . . .'

Everyone looked around the campsite. In its great circle of light, surrounded by a much greater darkness. The half-moon had disappeared from the night sky, along with all the stars. If the generator should fail and the lights stopped working . . . we would be left alone in the dark until morning.

'How tough is your generator?' I asked the Professor. 'How much damage could it take and still keep working?'

'I don't know,' said the Professor. 'But how could anything get to it without us noticing?'

'Something was moving around the camp in the dark,' said Penny. 'How do we know it isn't still out there?'

The scientists moved closer together, almost unconsciously, as they looked out at the darkness.

'I think we'd better keep the fire going,' I said. 'Just in case.'

'One small camp fire isn't going to be enough to light the whole of the site,' said Mike.

'We could always set fire to the tents . . .' I said.

Mike scowled at me. 'I can never tell when you're joking.'

'We can't worry about everything that could happen, or we'll never get anything done,' the Professor said briskly. 'Let's concentrate on what's in front of us. Mike, unclip the

cage and run some tests on it. See if there are any traces
left on the metal. Whatever smashed the lock might have left
something of itself behind.'

'Oh, come on!' said Mike. 'I checked all the other cages
this happened to and couldn't find anything. Why do I have
to do all the shit work?'

'Because you're annoying,' said the Professor. 'Get on
with it.'

'I'll help you, Mike,' said Ellie.

Mike gave us all his best martyred look, removed the steel
clasp, then carried the cage back to the equipment centre.
Ellie went with him and sat down beside him as he examined
the cage. They murmured quietly together. Paul went back
to the drum, to rewind the last of the cable.

'I'll take a look at the recording of the camera's descent,'
said the Professor. 'See if I can learn something from it.'

'Good idea,' I said.

Penny and I followed her back down the hill. When we
entered the equipment centre, Mike and Ellie made a point of
not looking up from what they were doing. The Professor
pulled up a chair before the monitor screen and started up the
recording. Only to find there wasn't one. Either it had been
wiped, or conditions inside the hole had simply been too alien
to make an impression. The Professor jumped to her feet,
kicked her chair aside, stormed out of the centre and strode
off towards the tents. I looked at Penny and we shrugged,
pretty much in unison.

'You want to take another look at the hole?' I said.

'Why not?' said Penny.

We marched back up the hill and stared thoughtfully at the
hole. Careful to stay well behind the safety line. The hole
didn't appear to have changed in any way.

'What are you looking for?' said Penny, slipping an arm
through mine.

'Something . . .' I said. 'Anything . . .'

'Well,' said Penny, 'at least now we can be sure that there
really is something in there.'

'But we don't have anything to connect it with any of the
deaths,' I said.

'You're not still thinking they might have been accidents?'

'No,' I said. 'Mike was right. I'd accept two as coincidence, three deaths have to mean enemy action. But I'm still half-convinced someone could be using the hole as a distraction, to disguise cold-blooded murder.'

'Just once, it would be nice to work on a simple straightforward case,' Penny said wistfully.

'If the case was simple and straightforward, we wouldn't be here,' I said.

'All right,' said Penny. 'Let's talk through the possibilities. What if one of the scientists is working with whatever's inside the hole?'

'How would they have made a deal?' I said. 'Its ideas of making contact suggest it doesn't want anything to do with humans.'

I broke off, as the Professor came trudging up the hill to join us. She glared at the hole as though it had let her down by being unfathomable.

'Is there any way we could seal off the hole?' asked Penny, tactfully changing the subject even before it had been raised. 'Make it impossible for anything to get out?'

'No,' the Professor said shortly.

'When Mr Carroll calls, you could ask for some workmen and a whole bunch of concrete,' said Penny.

'We tried covering the hole when we first arrived,' the Professor said heavily. 'To prevent anything from affecting or contaminating the surface. That was back when we thought the hole needed protecting from us. First we put a sheet over it, and then a tarpaulin. But the moment we turned our backs, the coverings just vanished. Sucked in by the hole. That was why we put down the safety line, to remind everyone to keep their distance. Because we couldn't trust the hole to be just a hole.'

'You don't think a covering of solid concrete would make any difference?' I said.

The Professor shook her head dismissively. 'You've felt the gravity that thing can generate.'

'What if we covered the hole with one of the tents?' said

Penny, just a bit desperately. 'Then if something was trying to fight its way through it we'd at least have some warning.'

'The tent would only go the same way as everything else,' said the Professor. 'And we're short enough of tents as it is.'

Penny looked to me for help. I looked calmly back at her. I was interested to see where she'd go next.

'All right,' said Penny. 'How about lateral thinking? What if you dug up the part of the hill that has the hole in it and transported it somewhere else? To some secure Black Heir laboratory where they could surround it with first-class equipment and a whole bunch of soldiers with really big guns?'

'I already thought of that,' said Paul.

I jumped a little, because I hadn't heard him come up behind us. And I should have. I was starting to feel seriously concerned about how much I was missing. My senses were letting me down.

Paul moved in beside the Professor, and looked at the hole as though it was an equation that refused to add up. 'The first time I scanned the hole, the readings made it clear the hole wasn't actually there, as such. It's not a hole in the hill. Mike already proved that by tunnelling beneath it. Basically, the hole is an overlay, imposed on top of our reality. If we were to dig up this particular piece of hillside and cart it away, I'm pretty sure the hole would still be there, hovering in mid-air.'

'Why didn't you tell me this before?' said the Professor.

'Because I've been trying to put together a report that wouldn't make me sound crazy,' said Paul.

'I want to see that report as soon as it's ready,' said the Professor.

'It's on my list of things to do,' said Paul.

I could see an argument was about to happen, so I caught Penny's eye and we walked off down the hill, leaving them to it. We went back inside the equipment centre and joined Mike and Ellie at their workbench, where they were still examining the specimen cage. This seemed to consist mostly of poking it with things to see what would happen.

'Find anything interesting?' I said.

'No physical traces of any kind left on the metal,' said Mike, not looking round. 'Just like all the other cages.'

'No chemical traces and no radiation,' said Ellie. 'Nothing to suggest anything about where it's been.'

'And my camera's gone,' said Mike, just a bit sulkily. 'I paid a lot of money for that camera . . .'

'Was it insured?' Penny asked politely.

Mike smiled for the first time. 'What do you suggest I put on the claim form?'

'Lost in action?' said Penny.

Ellie got to her feet and moved over to the plastic wall. She stretched slowly, taking her time. Mike watched her, reasonably unobtrusively, but I was pretty sure Ellie knew. That was why she'd done it right in front of him. She looked out at the darkness.

'How much longer before we can expect a call from Mr Carroll?'

'Hours and hours,' said Mike. He got up and moved in beside Ellie, looking at her rather than the dark. 'I hate being up this early in the morning. It's not natural. But it's not like I could sleep, anyway.'

'I don't know if I'll ever sleep again,' said Ellie. 'If I'll ever feel safe enough just to close my eyes.'

'I'm here,' said Mike. 'I'll protect you.'

'How?' Ellie said flatly. 'We don't even know what it is that's killing us.'

'I think we should all go back and sit by the fire,' I said, diplomatically. 'It's getting cold.'

Mike and Ellie didn't say anything, but they allowed Penny and me to lead the way back down the hill. The camp fire was still burning steadily, its flames untroubled by even a breath of moving air. Which was odd. There should have been some wind blowing, halfway up a hill as steep as this one . . . But I hadn't felt so much as a breeze since we got here. Mike and Ellie dropped down heavily by the fire, almost but not quite leaning against each other for support. Penny and I sat down on the opposite side of the fire, and we all sat together in a silence that might have been uncomfortable if we hadn't all been so tired. After a while, Paul and the Professor came to join us. They didn't have anything to say either, having apparently argued each other to a draw.

'I hate this place,' Mike said suddenly. He couldn't summon up enough energy to put the proper amount of venom into his voice, but we all nodded, ready to take the thought for the deed.

'It could be worse,' I said.

'How?' said Mike.

'It could be raining.'

The old joke didn't raise a smile from anyone. Not even Penny.

'At least we're not hearing anything moving around in the dark any more,' she said finally.

'You had to remind us, didn't you?' said Ellie. 'Like I wasn't jumpy enough already. Though with the mood I'm in right now, if something did appear suddenly out of the dark I would kick the living crap out of it.'

'I thought you were tired,' said Mike.

'Not that tired,' said Ellie. They managed a small smile for each other.

Since casual conversation clearly wasn't going to get us anywhere, I took it upon myself to be the voice of reason. Because somebody had to.

'If we do hear anything out in the night, I don't want anyone going off to investigate it on their own,' I said sternly. 'We're perfectly safe as long as we all stay together in the light.'

'What if something comes into the light?' said Mike.

'I'll protect you,' I said steadily.

'And just how are you going to do that?' said Ellie. 'We don't know what's out there, or what's in the hole, or what's trying to kill us.'

'Well . . .' said Mike. 'Whatever it is, it can't be that powerful.'

Ellie looked at him. 'Explain.'

'If it was really dangerous, it wouldn't need to hide in the dark, would it?' Mike said reasonably. 'It wouldn't be sneaking around, picking us off one by one. It would just come straight at us and kill us all.'

'Is that supposed to reassure me?' said Ellie.

'I don't know,' said Mike. 'Maybe.'

He tried to put an arm around her, but she shrugged him

off. Mike quietly withdrew his arm, and gave his full attention to the fire. Paul looked thoughtfully at the tent holding Terry and Robert's bodies. I hadn't told anyone that I'd forced Robert's body into the same sleeping bag as Terry, and then jammed the zip to make sure they wouldn't be getting out. I didn't think the other scientists needed to know that. But when Paul looked at the tent, everyone else did too. The Professor looked like she was about to say something caustic, so Penny jumped in quickly to forestall her.

'Professor Bellman, you said earlier that there were a lot of local stories about old-time disappearances in this area. Can you tell us more about them?'

She shot me a look to keep quiet and let the Professor tell us what she knew. I didn't mind. I never claimed to be an expert on the area. The Professor nodded slowly.

'I was given a pretty hefty briefing file to read on the drive here. Old legends and the like. At the time I put it all down to local superstitions, but now I'm not so sure. Some of it is starting to make a disturbing sort of sense. There were a great many stories about fairy rings on Brassknocker Hill. Perfect circles in the grass that appeared out of nowhere, their boundaries marked by unfamiliar flowers and toadstools with unsettling markings.

'The local people decided they were bad places and had the good sense to stay well clear of them. There were all kinds of cautionary tales, about people who stepped inside the fairy rings and found themselves transported to other worlds, where sometimes the very rules of reality were different. Full of creatures that only looked like human beings, with behaviour and rituals that seemed almost a parody of human behaviour. Some of these missing people returned after spending only a single night in this otherworldly place to find decades or even centuries had passed, and everyone they knew was dead and gone. As though time itself moved differently in these other realities.

'There were also a great many stories about people who set off to travel at night, for perfectly good and necessary reasons, but never got to where they were going. They just vanished between one place and the next, never to be seen or heard of again. According to the Black Heir file, Brassknocker Hill holds the record for the highest number of unexplained missing people in the whole country, and always has. Down the years these disappearances have been blamed on everything from fairies to demon dogs, from Beasts to flying saucers. There are all kinds of books on the subject, by people keen to press their own particular brand of paranoia.'

The Professor then told a version of the story I'd told Penny earlier, about the young man who left his family cottage one night, cried out, and vanished. But the Professor had her own disturbing coda to add.

'The family rushed out into the night, only to find the young man's footsteps stopped right in the middle of a huge snow-covered field. And when they listened, they could hear the young man's voice crying out for help . . . from somewhere high up in the sky. Growing gradually fainter, as it drifted away into some unimaginable distance.'

There was a pause, as everyone looked at each other.

'Thanks a whole bunch,' said Ellie. 'I already knew I was never going to sleep again without industrial-strength chemical assistance. Now I've got to worry about something snatching me up and carrying me away!'

'All of these stories can be interpreted as people encountering holes in the world, similar to ours,' said the Professor. 'Which suggests that the appearance and disappearance of such holes is a recurring phenomenon, going back centuries.'

'If these holes are potential invasion points,' said Mike, 'why don't they appear in the middle of cities, where they could see more and do more damage?'

'Maybe they just don't want to be noticed yet,' said Ellie.

'All we have to do is wait, and the hole will vanish,' the Professor said firmly. 'Taking its threat with it.'

'It can't disappear soon enough to suit me,' said Mike.

'But why do these holes keep appearing?' said Penny. 'If the hole's an invasion point, where's the invasion? Why do the holes always seem to settle for kidnapping the occasional passer-by?'

'I think they're just spy holes,' said Paul. 'So their makers can study us from a safe distance and learn all about us.'

'That's almost a more worrying thought than an invasion,' said Mike. 'Alien voyeurs . . .'

'What about the Beast?' said Ellie. 'Nobody's mentioned the Beast. Why send something like that through the hole?'

'We sent test animals in,' said the Professor. 'Perhaps they send the Beast so it can grab people and take them back to its world. To be . . . examined.'

'So now we're talking alien abductions?' said Ellie. 'Dragging people away to be dissected?'

'I won't let anyone hurt you, Ellie,' said Mike.

She turned on him sharply. 'And how would you stop them?'

'I would stand between you and all harm,' said Mike.

Ellie looked at him for a long moment, and then her expression slowly softened.

'You would, wouldn't you?'

'You know I would,' said Mike.

Ellie smiled at him, and he smiled back. She took his hand in hers, and he held on to it like it was something infinitely precious.

'We just have to wait the hole out,' the Professor said flatly. 'Once it's gone, we'll be safe.'

'When the hole disappears, so do all our chances of career-making discoveries,' said Paul.

'I can live with that,' said Mike.

Ellie stood up suddenly, jerking her hand out of his. 'I'm going to my tent. I have to try to get some sleep. I don't think I've ever felt this tired in my life.'

Mike rose quickly to his feet. 'I'll go with you.'

'You'd both be a lot safer staying here,' I said steadily. 'Where we can all keep an eye on each other. It's not that long till morning.'

'I know,' said Ellie. 'But I can't keep my eyes open, and I don't want to nod off sitting by the fire. That feels . . . far too vulnerable. At least, in my tent I'll have some walls around me.'

'I could join you,' said Mike. 'Watch over you while you sleep.'

She looked at him, and then smiled warmly as she saw he really meant it.

'Thank you, Mike, but no. It's just too soon, after Robert.'

'I could sit outside your tent on guard,' said Mike. 'Make sure you are safe, because anything would have to get through me to get to you.'

'You look more exhausted than me,' Ellie said kindly. 'Go to your own tent and get some sleep, Mike. We'll talk more in the morning.'

She took hold of his face with both hands, pulled him gently forward, and kissed him on the forehead. Then she walked over to her tent, and went inside without looking back once. Mike watched her all the way, just in case, and then went into his tent. Paul rose unhurriedly to his feet.

'I'm going to take one last look at my instruments, check the readings. See if there are any changes in the hole or its surroundings after everything that's happened. And when I've done that, I'm going to get some sleep. I want to be sharp for the radio call.'

He walked up the hill to the equipment centre, leaving just the Professor sitting by the fire with Penny and me. She waited until she was sure Paul was out of earshot, and then fixed me with a steady gaze.

'This investigation was my last chance to be a success, and it's all gone wrong.' She shook her head slowly. 'I have to salvage something from this mess . . . Because the next generation of hot young things is never far behind. The scientific community is supposed to be all about adding new things to Humanity's store of knowledge . . . But in reality it's always "What have you done recently?". And unless it's big enough and new enough, they throw you on the scrapheap without even a second thought for who you used to be. I'm damned if I'll go quietly into the long night of retirement! Not while my mind is still sharp.

'I'm going to take one last look at Terry and Robert's notes, see if there might be anything significant in them that we missed. Then I think I'll get some sleep, too. It's been a long day. And night.' She looked at me coldly. 'Feel free to stay on guard. That worked so well the last time.'

She heaved herself up on to her feet and headed for the equipment centre. She passed Paul coming back, heading for the tents, and they murmured quietly to each other before continuing on their way. Penny looked at me.

'It's good that these people feel they can unburden themselves to us.'

'I thought so,' I said.

'Is it just me, or did the Professor seem a bit despondent?
And really, really bitter?'

'Disillusioned, certainly, when it comes to the academic
world. And definitely bitter about what's happened to her
career . . . But to be honest, I'm getting that from all of them.
A sense that all their careers were going down for the third
time, and this investigation was their lifeline. They weren't
only chosen because they were geniuses. It mattered just as
much that they were desperate. And possibly, expendable.'

'Like us!' said Penny.

'Oh, that goes without saying in our line of work. But I
don't think anyone here was ever going to get what they
wanted. There are no Nobel Prizes to be found in that hole.
It's just a mystery that may possibly be beyond human
comprehension.'

'Are you including yourself in that?' said Penny.

'Yes,' I said. 'I've seen my share of marvels and mysteries,
horrible things and terrible places . . . And sometimes the
smartest thing you can do is walk away.'

'I don't think we have that option here,' said Penny. 'We
need to figure this mystery out, or there's a real possibility
none of us will be here by morning.'

I looked at the tents. 'You know, just once on these kind of
cases . . . Just once I wish that when I tell people to stay
together they'd stay together. It's not rocket science! It's always
the ones who go off on their own who end up getting killed.
Why does no one ever listen to me?'

'Because you're always too reasonable with them,' said
Penny. 'People don't respond well to reason.'

'Humans!' I growled.

'We could always discuss mating rituals . . .' said Penny.

'Later,' I said.

We sat together for a while, listening to the crackle of the
flames in the fire and the unnervingly complete quiet of
the night outside the camp's circle of light.

'It's hard to come up with any plans,' I said finally, 'when

we can't even be sure what it is we're fighting. Or if there
actually is anything to fight. All we know for sure is that two
scientists have died. I am seriously considering phoning the
Colonel and having him send me a really nasty bomb, so I
can drop it into the hole.'

'To blow up the hole?' said Penny.

'No,' I said. 'To persuade whatever's at the bottom of the
hole to stop messing with us.'

'Ishmael,' Penny said carefully, 'is there any particular
reason why you're so reluctant to call the Colonel? I know
you don't like asking for help, but wouldn't we be better off
with a small army of heavily armed reinforcements to secure
the site and protect these people?'

'I'm not phoning the Colonel,' I said, just as carefully,
'because he told me not to. Apparently there's some big head-
butting jurisdictional fight going on, between the Organization
and Black Heir, as to who should have control over the hole.
I don't know any more than that, because that's all the Colonel
told me. Except . . . that while the Organization and Black
Heir might be co-operating for the moment, that could change
at any time.

'The Colonel was very firm that I shouldn't do anything
that might make the Organization appear weak. If I admit
failure and call for help, Black Heir could use that as an excuse
to kick the two of us out and put in their own people. And
the Colonel informed me that if that were to happen the
Organization might well decide they don't need my services
any more . . . I would be cut loose and set adrift, with no
more protection from the suspicious and inquisitive world.'

'They can't just let you go!' said Penny. 'Not after everything you've done for them!'

'Of course they can,' I said. 'The only thing the Organization
and I have ever had in common is that we're useful to each
other.'

Penny looked at me for a long moment. 'Would you really
put these people's lives at risk rather than lose the Organization's
protection?'

'No,' I said. 'But what if I make the call and the Colonel
says things don't sound bad enough to justify sending any

help? I'm not the only one who doesn't want to look bad to the Organization. I can't call him until I've got something important enough to compel him to take action.'

Penny shook her head slowly. 'I always thought the Organization was above that kind of petty politics.'

'Me too,' I said. 'But when you get right down to it, the Organization has to work alongside all the other secret groups that deal with cases of the weird and uncanny. Mostly they all stick to their own particular areas of expertise, but there are bound to be cases where they're ready to clash over some particularly tasty prize. Of course, no one wants a civil war . . . unless they can be sure they'll win. And let's be honest, Penny, what good would reinforcements do, anyway? By the time they could get here, any number of things could have happened – including the hole's disappearance. We're the ones best suited to working out what the hell is going on here.'

'You know, for someone who isn't a scientist, you do talk a lot of sense sometimes,' said Paul.

I looked up with a start. I hadn't heard him stop off to listen to us, on his way to the tents.

'Something we can do for you, Paul?' I asked, just a bit pointedly.

'I've done all I can for now,' said Paul. 'The hole is behaving itself, and I've got to get some sleep before I collapse. Has the Professor come back yet?'

'Where from?' said Penny.

'She said she was going to take one last look at the hole before turning in,' said Paul.

I quickly rose to my feet, and so did Penny. I looked up the hill to the hole, starkly illuminated by its extra lights. There was no sign of the Professor.

'She couldn't have been that stupid, could she?' said Penny. 'To go there on her own after everything that's happened?'

'There's something about the hole,' I said. 'It gets to people.'

Penny looked quickly around her. 'I don't see her anywhere.'

I headed for the hole, and Penny and Paul hurried after me.

'The Professor was determined to get something out of this investigation while the hole's still here,' I said, not looking back at the others because I didn't want to take my eyes off the hole. 'She needed something she could present to the Government to justify her presence here. But what could she have been planning to do?'

'Probably something desperate,' said Paul. 'Because what else has she got?'

I felt a sudden urgency and pressed on ahead, leaving Penny and Paul behind. When I got to the hole, it looked exactly the same. No sign that the Professor had been there, or tried to do anything. Penny and Paul caught up with me, and we all stood together, well behind the safety line. The hole stared calmly back at us, its flat black surface giving nothing away.

'She couldn't have gone in, could she?' said Penny.

'She didn't cross the line,' I said. 'Look at the grass in front of the hole. No fresh footprints.'

'You've got good eyes,' said Paul.

'Usually,' I said.

'Can you see any traces in the grass to show where the Professor might have gone after she left here?' said Penny.

I looked, but the whole area had been so trampled over it was impossible to make out anything.

'We have to find the Professor,' I said, 'and make sure she hasn't done anything stupid. Or dangerous.'

I led the way back down the hillside. The camp lay open and empty before us, brightly illuminated by the perimeter lights. There was no sign of the Professor anywhere.

'Maybe she's inside her tent,' said Penny.

'She would have had to pass right by us when we were sitting beside the fire,' I said. 'And I didn't see or hear anything.'

Penny looked at me. She didn't say anything, because she didn't need to. It was becoming clearer all the time that my senses weren't as sharp as usual.

'Could the Beast have sneaked into the camp and carried away the Professor?' said Paul.

'I would definitely have noticed that,' I said.

When we finally reached the tents I looked at Paul, and he pointed to the one on the far left. I strode over to it, ripped open the flaps, and stuck my head in. There was just enough light for me to make out a single sleeping bag, opened but not slept in. No personal belongings, not even a change of clothes.

That's what happens when a secret Government department drags you away to work for them without any warning. I stepped back, let the flaps close, and looked at Penny and Paul.

'She's not in there.'

'Could she have left the site?' said Paul. 'Maybe tried to get to your car?'

'It's locked,' Penny said immediately. 'And I've got the keys.' She stopped, and slapped her pocket hard to hear them jingle. Just to reassure herself. And then she frowned, and looked out into the dark. 'Perhaps she heard something moving around, like we did earlier. But she'd have had more sense than to go out into the dark on her own, wouldn't she?'

We moved over to the nearest part of the perimeter and stood between two lights, looking out into the night. It looked back at us, cold and silent and unfathomable. I couldn't see a thing, and when I strained my hearing against the hush I couldn't hear anything either. Penny looked at me.

'You are *not* going out into the dark after the Professor,' she said flatly.

'I wasn't planning to,' I said. 'Not without some evidence that she's out there.'

'There's nowhere left to look in the camp,' said Paul.

'Maybe she's in the toilet,' said Penny.

We looked past the tents, to the single portable cabin. The door was hanging open.

'All right,' said Penny. 'Maybe she sneaked into one of the other tents.'

'I'm pretty sure Mike or Ellie would have made one hell of a fuss about that,' I said.

'What if she wanted to look at the bodies?' said Paul.

We inspected the tent where I'd put Terry and Robert.

'The tent flaps are still closed,' I said. 'She would have had to leave them open if she was still inside.'

'She has to be somewhere!' said Penny.

A woman screamed, shrill and piercing, and then the sound cut off abruptly. I spun round, to look at the hole. And all I could think was: *Something's got out . . .*

Mike's head emerged from his tent, bleary-eyed and confused.

'What is it? What's happening?'

'Something's happened at the hole,' I said. 'Stay here!'

I sprinted up the hill. Paul and Penny hurried after me, but I soon left them behind. I could hear Mike calling Ellie's name outside her tent, but there was no reply.

When I got to the hole, the Professor was standing over another body, her face full of shock and horror. It took me a moment to understand the body was Ellie's, because the head was gone. Not just removed: there was no sign of it anywhere. And just like Robert's missing arm, despite the severity of the injury the wound was unnaturally smooth and there wasn't a trace of blood anywhere on the grass surrounding the hole.

Penny and Paul finally arrived, struggling to get their breath. Penny made a low sound as she saw the headless body, and grabbed hold of my arm. Paul just stood there. Mike arrived a few moments later, breathing hard.

'Ellie's missing!' he said. 'She's not in her tent!'

'We know,' I said, as gently as I could.

Mike looked at the headless body. He tried to say something, but couldn't. As though all the breath had been punched out of him. He dropped to his knees beside Ellie and started to cry, great heaving sobs that shook his whole body. Penny put a comforting hand on his shoulder, but he didn't even know she was there. I turned to the Professor, and she started talking without taking her eyes off the headless body.

'I went to Ellie's tent, because I'd had a marvellous new insight I wanted to discuss with her, but the tent was empty. I was heading back to the equipment centre, to check out my idea, when I heard something moving up by the hole. By the time I got here, Ellie was already dead.'

I stopped listening, intent on my own thoughts. How did Ellie leave her tent and get past me without my noticing? Why did she leave her tent in the first place, though she said she was exhausted? And why come to the hole, after what it did to Robert? Did it call her? Or did someone persuade her to go?

'Why didn't anyone stop her?' said Mike. He'd stopped himself crying through an effort of will. His voice was so steady it sounded almost emotionless.

'We don't yet know what happened,' I said. 'I think you should go back to the fire, Mike, while we try to work this out.'

'I don't want to go,' said Mike. 'I don't want to leave her.'

'I know,' I said. 'But there's nothing you can do. She's gone.'

I looked at Penny, and she tried to help Mike to his feet. But she couldn't move him. Paul stepped in to help, and between them they got Mike on his feet and heading back down the hill to the fire. He didn't have the strength to fight them.

'You should go with them,' I said to the Professor.

She shook her head. 'I need to understand what happened. You were supposed to be on guard! How did she get past you?'

'It's the hole,' I said steadily. 'It has to be the hole. Just by being here, this unnatural thing forced into our reality is affecting everything around it. Messing with our minds and our senses . . . None of us have been thinking clearly. The hole is hiding things from us.'

The Professor flinched at the anger in my voice. She turned away to look at the headless body again.

'We are sure this is Ellie? I mean, without a head . . .'

'Those are her clothes,' I said. 'And this close, I can smell her scent.'

'Her perfume?'

'More than that,' I said.

She looked at me, puzzled, but didn't press the point. I knelt down beside the body. The neck had been severed with impossible precision; there was nothing to indicate the teeth or claws of a Beast at work. It had to be the result of sudden contact with the edge of the hole. Just like Robert. There were no signs of damage anywhere else on the body and no defensive wounds to the hands or arms, which suggested she never got a chance to protect herself. But why would Ellie go so close to the hole, after what happened to Robert? She'd been so disturbed by his death, and the manner of it, that I would have bet good money she'd never go near the hole again.

'What was she doing here?' said the Professor.

'I think somebody brought her here,' I said, getting to my

feet. 'Someone went to Ellie's tent, woke her up, and persuaded her to come here.'

'Why would she go?' said the Professor.

'Either this other person was very convincing, or it was someone she trusted,' I said. 'But who could it have been? I was with Penny. And Paul was with us when she screamed. So that just leaves Mike – who came out of his tent right after the scream – and you. Where were you, Professor? We looked all over for you.'

'Ellie wasn't the one who screamed,' she said quietly. 'It was me. It was just such a shock . . .'

'But where were you before that?' I said.

'I went to check the generator was working properly,' she said. 'After what you said about how defenceless we'd be if the lights went out, I thought I should check. It's set up some distance behind the tents. That's why you didn't see me.'

I let that pass, for the moment. I hadn't been seeing a lot of things.

'Ellie would have trusted Mike,' I said. 'She might have come here with him, if he'd asked. But why would he do something like this?'

'He wanted her to love him,' said the Professor. 'We all saw that. Maybe she decided she didn't. So he brought her here . . .'

'But how could he have persuaded her to go somewhere she was so afraid of?'

'To face her fear?' said the Professor. 'Particularly if she was having trouble sleeping. Mike would understand how her mind worked.'

'So would Paul,' I said. 'He could have asked her for help with a scientific problem. He was with me when we heard the scream, but since that was you no one has an alibi . . . And then there's you, Professor. We couldn't find you anywhere, and you had the authority to order her to go with you to the hole.'

'Why would I do that?' said the Professor.

'I don't know,' I said. 'Is there anything you want to tell me, Professor?'

'Yes,' she said, looking at the hole. 'I'm cold and I'm tired. So very tired.'

I looked down at Ellie's body. What did happen here? Did Ellie stick her head into the hole, to see for herself what was happening inside it, and something took her head? Or could someone have brought her here in order to push her against the edge of the hole? Was there a cold-blooded murderer in the camp, picking off the members of the team one by one, using the hole as a murder weapon and a distraction?

Or was something coming up out of the hole and killing people for its own unknowable reasons?

So many theories, so many questions. And I couldn't choose between them, because I had no clues and no evidence to work with. Anyone could be guilty. Or nobody.

'You have to solve this,' said the Professor.

'I know,' I said, not looking around.

'No,' she said. 'I mean, you have to solve this as a matter of urgency. Because I've noticed that every time one of us dies, the hole gets just a little bit bigger.'

FOUR

Some People Have a Beast in Them and Vice Versa

I looked at the Professor for a long moment. 'It's bigger? Are you sure?'

'Of course I'm sure!'

'How much bigger?'

'Not much,' the Professor said steadily. 'But a measurable amount.'

'And you think that's connected with the people who have died here?'

'I can't prove it. But if it isn't, that would be a hell of a coincidence. I have to wonder if perhaps we're feeding the hole. Paying it tribute, in blood and death.'

'How would that work?' I said.

'I don't know!' the Professor said loudly. 'I don't feel like I understand anything about the hole any more. Except that it scares the crap out of me.'

I nodded slowly.

'For now, keep this to yourself, Professor. We can't prove anything, and people are scared enough as it is.'

She shrugged, and then made herself look at the headless body again. 'What are you going to do with Ellie?'

'Put her somewhere safe,' I said.

I knelt down beside Ellie again. It had been a long time since I'd felt this helpless on a case. I'd had such good intentions when I came here. This was going to be the case where I protected everyone so well that no one had to die. You'd think I'd know better than to make such promises to myself.

I cradled Ellie's body in my arms and got to my feet. Not a single drop of blood fell from the severed neck, as though the hole's gravity had sucked all the blood out of her. Just like when Robert lost his arm. So if there was a killer, it was no wonder I hadn't seen any incriminating bloodstains on anyone's clothing. Yet another clue I didn't have to work with. But was the blood loss down to gravity, or because the hole was hungry?

Ellie's body felt oddly unbalanced in my arms, without a head. I held her close to me, even though it was too late to protect her from anything. I walked back down the hillside into the camp, and the Professor trudged along behind me. Not weeping, not saying a word. I could still feel her presence at my back, like a silent reproach.

When I got to the camp fire, Penny, Mike and Paul all looked up as I walked past, carrying my burden. Penny looked at me steadily, making it clear she didn't judge me. Paul looked at Ellie, not at me. Mike looked like he wanted to say something, but didn't know what. His angry eyes burned holes in my back as I headed for the tents. The Professor sat down beside the fire with the others, still not saying anything.

I stopped outside the tent where I'd put Terry and Robert. I held Ellie's body to me with one arm while I opened the flaps with the other. Then I paused for a moment, half-convinced that when I went in I'd find the other two bodies were gone. That someone had taken advantage of the situation to remove them while I was preoccupied. Or even worse, I would step inside the tent to find Terry and Robert were no longer in their sleeping bag. But just standing there waiting for me . . .

Smiling.

I'd seen stranger things, on other cases. Death isn't always as final as most people think.

I shouldered my way in past the tent flaps. Ready to drop Ellie in a moment if I had to defend myself. But even in the deep gloom of the tent's interior, I could still make out the two bodies filling the sleeping bag. Stuffed in together, back to back, just as I'd left them. That had seemed more respectful than face to face. I laid Ellie down beside the sleeping bag, and then gave the zipper a good hard tug, just to make sure it was still firmly jammed. It didn't budge an inch. No one was going to get that bag open in a hurry. Not even Terry and Robert.

I looked around the tent, straining my eyes against the

shadows. There was nothing else I could use to stop Ellie from
getting up and going for a walk, if she felt so inclined. And
no way I could force a third body into the sleeping bag. So I
just left her lying on the tent floor. At least without a head,
she'd have a hard time finding any victims, since she wouldn't
be able to see where she was going. I allowed myself a small
smile. Sometimes graveyard humour is all we have to help us
cope. I went to leave, and then hesitated and looked back. At
the three people I couldn't keep from being killed. There
wasn't anything I could say, so I just nodded to them and left
the tent.

I tucked the flaps back into place, and then stood outside the
tent, looking up and down the hillside and all around the brightly
illuminated campsite. There was no sign of life or movement
anywhere, apart from the four people sitting round the fire. It
infuriated me that after everything that had happened I still
hadn't caught even a glimpse of our mystery killer, whether it
was a man or a Beast. There was never any warning, no sign
of imminent danger, nothing to suggest anyone was at risk.
The killer just came and went, and killed, and no one ever saw
anything. So either I was dealing with a real professional, or
a real monster. Either way, I was missing something.

I looked at the people sitting silently round the fire. It was
always possible the killer was hiding in plain sight, and I
was looking right at the killer. But how could I point the finger
at anyone, when there was no clear motive, never mind hard
evidence? Mike could have attacked Robert so that he could
have Ellie for himself. But she'd already said she was thinking
of leaving Robert for Mike. And why would Mike kill his
beloved Ellie in such an appalling fashion after doing so much
to win her? Unless she told him she didn't want him after all.
After everything he'd done. I could see him striking out at her
then in a fit of blind fury.

But what about Terry? I might have been ready to accept
his death as happenstance, if he'd been the only one. But not
now there were two more deaths associated with the hole. At
the very least, someone must have secretly encouraged Terry
to go into the hole. And why would Mike want to hurt Terry?

He'd never even met the man before he came here. Unless the killing wasn't about the man, but about the hole. What if Terry's death really had been a terrible accident, and Mike had taken advantage of it to draw attention away from his own murders?

I shook my head. I was having a hard time seeing Mike as a cold-blooded murderer. A hot-blooded one, in the heat of the moment, maybe . . . But Robert would never have let Mike get close enough to push him against the hole's edge. At the very least there would have been a struggle, and I hadn't seen any signs of that in the grass near the hole.

I frowned, as a new thought occurred to me. The use of the hole's razor-sharp edges suggested a weapon of opportunity. If the killings had been planned in advance, the killer would have found some way to smuggle in a weapon. It seemed far more likely that something happened here, at the camp, to turn one of the scientists into a killer. But what could be so important, so overwhelming, that one of these people had been driven to kill so horribly again and again? Did the choice of the hole as a weapon say something about the killer? Only that whoever it was had to be very determined. Any of the scientists could have used the hole as a weapon; it wouldn't have taken any special strength or skill.

Even the Professor could have done it. But why would she want to? She needed her team to do the work, to get the discoveries she needed to restart her career. And she didn't know any of them well enough to have a personal grudge. Unless the hole had affected her mind. I was certain it was messing with me, damping my senses back to an almost human level. But then why wasn't the hole driving all of them crazy?

I thought about Paul. The quiet-spoken one, who only seemed to care about his work. In my line of work, it's always the quiet ones you have to watch out for. They always turn out to have the mostly deeply hidden motives, and emotions that blaze up out of control when they finally break loose. But I couldn't see any reason why Paul would want to kill anyone. Unless he wanted the hole for himself, so he would get sole credit when he finally unlocked its mysteries . . .

I'd been standing outside the tent for quite a while, lost in my own thoughts, and I suddenly realized the others were looking at me curiously, even suspiciously. I smiled easily at them, as though I'd just been wool-gathering, walked over to the fire and sat down beside Penny.

The surviving members of the scientific team all looked shocked, in their various ways. The Professor was wringing her hands together, perhaps to keep them from shaking. The lines in her face looked deeper than ever, and her eyes were full of a quiet desperation. She stared into the quietly crackling flames, intent on something only she could see, ignoring everything else.

Paul seemed almost relaxed by comparison, ignoring the fire and the people sitting around it, staring out across the empty campsite at the darkness beyond the perimeter lights. He seemed lost in his own thoughts, and I couldn't read any of them in his blank impassive face. Perhaps he just didn't know what to do.

Mike had moved beyond grief and shock and into anger. He scowled openly at me, and I had no trouble recognizing the look in his eyes. He needed someone to blame, someone to take out his pain on; and in the absence of the murderer, he'd settle for me. I would have to be careful around Mike from now on, because he was just looking for an excuse to lash out. Because he thought that would make him feel better. Of all those left in the camp, Mike was the most obviously dangerous. In an entirely hot-blooded kind of way.

I looked at Penny, and found she was looking anxiously at me. It took me a moment to realize it was because I was thinking so much and saying nothing. I smiled at her reassuringly, and then cleared my throat loudly. Everyone looked at me, silently demanding answers. Or at the very least, some kind of comfort or reassurance. I sighed internally. I'd never been any good at faking that kind of thing.

'Do I really need to tell you that the hole is off limits to everyone, from now on?' I said steadily. 'It's simply too dangerous.'

'The hole?' said Paul. 'Or whoever is using it to kill us?'

'Let's just say the hole, for now,' I said. 'No one is to go off on their own, for any reason. Stick together, and stay in sight of each other at all times. It should be dawn in a few more hours.'

Mike leaned forward the moment I stopped speaking, glad for a chance to challenge me over something.

'What if we need to get something from our tents?' he said sharply. 'Something we have to have?'

'Do without,' said Penny.

'What if one of us needs to use the toilet?' said the Professor.

'If anyone needs to go, we'll all go with them,' said Penny. 'And stand around outside till they've finished.'

'I can't do it if anybody's listening,' said the Professor.

'Then you'll just have to whistle loudly and think of something else,' I said.

'Why did you spend so long standing outside the tent?' said Paul. 'What were you thinking about?'

'What to do for the best,' I said.

Mike's anger flared up again. 'You should have let me carry Ellie down the hill. You had no right! Not after you failed to protect her.'

'You were in the tent right next to her,' I said steadily. 'Didn't you hear her leave and go off on her own?'

Mike scowled, and looked down at his hands. He didn't seem to know what to do with them. 'I was asleep the moment I lay down. I was just so tired . . . I should have sat on guard outside her tent, like I wanted.'

'You'd only have nodded off anyway,' Penny said kindly.

'Just my being there might have been enough,' he said. 'At least I could have stopped her going to the hole. Why would she do that?'

'I'm convinced someone persuaded Ellie to go with them to the hole,' I said. 'If you had been there, they might have taken you instead.'

'I would have gone,' said Mike. 'If that would have saved Ellie . . . I would have gone.'

'Don't think so much about death,' I said. 'You need to concentrate on staying alive. As long as we stick together . . .'

Mike flared up again, seizing on something else he could be angry about. 'You really expect us to stay here? After everything that's happened? Terry and Robert and Ellie are dead, and that archaeologist! We have to get out of here while we still can.'

Paul and the Professor looked at each other, considering the idea, then the Professor shook her head.

'If we leave, we lose everything,' she said quietly. 'No more access to the hole, none of the grant money we were promised, and no boost to our careers. All our work will be lost. No one will ever know we were here.'

'We'll be giving up our only opportunity to understand the mystery of the hole,' said Paul.

'I don't care!' Mike said loudly. 'It killed Ellie. It'll kill us all, if we stay.'

The Professor looked up the hillside, to the hole. We all followed her gaze. Sitting placidly on the side of the hill, the hole seemed such a small thing to be so dangerous.

'This is our only chance to understand what that thing really is,' the Professor said stubbornly. 'One of the great undiscovered wonders of the world, and it's ours. We have to grab hold of it with both hands, and wring the truth out of it while we can. Because the hole won't be here much longer. It'll vanish soon, just like all the others.'

'Not necessarily,' said Paul.

We all turned to look at him. It wasn't like him to be so blunt, so certain.

'What makes you think the hole won't disappear?' said the Professor. She sounded honestly curious.

'You proceed from false logic,' Paul said calmly. 'How do we know this hole is like any of the other holes that appeared before? I believe whoever has been sending these holes into our world has been working on improving them, until they could finally establish a permanent connection between their world and ours. Like Ellie said, a tunnel and an invasion point.'

'That's a lot of maybes,' I said. 'There's no evidence this hole is any different to the others.'

'There's no evidence it's the same,' said Paul.

'What kind of argument is that?' said Penny.

Mike snorted loudly. 'Wishful thinking. And in pretty bad taste, all things considered.'

'Well,' I said, 'since there isn't any evidence, let's go with

Occam's Razor and assume we're dealing with the same kind of hole. And hope this one will disappear like all the others.'

'Hope?' said Paul. 'That's what you're going with?'

'Don't you believe in hope?' said Penny.

'Of course not,' said Paul. 'I'm a scientist. I don't hope things will happen, I make them happen.'

'OK,' said Penny. 'A statement like that should really be accompanied by a dramatic crash of thunder and some lightning.'

'If we just sit around and wait for the hole to vanish, we'll all be dead before morning,' said Mike.

'I won't let that happen,' I said.

He just sneered at me. 'Yeah, right. Because you've done such a great job protecting us so far.'

I gave him a hard look, but he didn't back down. He was too angry to be intimidated. So I looked away, rather than give him an excuse to start something. I didn't want to have to hurt Mike, he'd been hurt enough already.

'What if something from inside the hole has been killing people?' said Paul. 'Could you defend us from something like that?'

'Do you have a gun?' the Professor said bluntly.

'No,' I said. 'I didn't think I'd need one.'

'Wonderful!' said Mike.

'So you can't defend us,' said Paul. 'Not from what we might be facing here.'

'Could you defend yourselves?' said Penny.

That stopped them. The scientists looked at each other uncertainly, as they considered the question.

Mike frowned. 'There must be something in the camp we could make into weapons.'

'All we have is what Black Heir provided,' said the Professor. She looked at Paul. 'You know the equipment best. Is there anything that could be adapted?'

'Not that I know of,' said Paul. 'Most of what we've got in the centre is pretty delicate stuff.'

'Yeah, but a lot of it comes in some pretty heavy housing,' said Mike. 'We could always bash someone over the head.'

'You really want to let the killer get that close?' said Paul.

I remembered my earlier thought, that the killer was only using the hole's edges as a weapon because there wasn't anything else.

Penny looked at Mike. 'You said you were ready to defend Ellie. What were you planning to use?'

He looked back at her with a certain dignity. 'I planned to stand in the way of anything that came for her. And then do my best to beat the living crap out of it.' He looked down at his hands, clenched into fists so tight the knuckles showed white. 'But I never got the chance to find out if I really was that brave.'

The Professor turned to me. 'Mike's not a fighter. He's a scientist, like all of us. Can you fight?'

'When I have to,' I said. 'That's part of the job.'

'Yes, Mister Big Secret Security Man,' said Mike. 'But what else are you?'

Something in his voice caught everyone's attention. He had the sound of someone who knew something, or thought he did.

'What are you talking about, Mike?' said the Professor.

Mike looked at me challengingly. 'I don't think he's who he says he is. And neither is his girlfriend.'

The Professor glared at Mike. 'We've already been through that! We have no way of checking up on them until Mr Carroll contacts us.'

'You didn't really think I was going to wait for that, did you?' said Mike. 'I did my own checking, on the computer.'

The Professor looked shocked. 'You should have checked with me before doing anything like that! I'm in charge of this team.'

'Only technically,' said Mike.

'You should have talked to me,' said Paul. 'I could have helped.'

'I didn't want anyone's help,' Mike said flatly. 'The only people I could be sure of in this camp were Ellie and Robert. Now they're dead, I don't trust anybody.'

'Well,' said Paul, 'at least now we all know where we stand.'

Penny looked thoughtfully at Mike. 'I thought you said

Black Heir controlled your access to the outside world? That you weren't allowed to talk to unauthorized people?'

Mike smiled. 'Oh, yes . . . Limited access to approved sites and people only, for security reasons. But you don't get to be genius scientists like us without learning your way around a computer. The good stuff is always going to be off limits, so you have to go and get it. It didn't take me ten minutes to break through the restrictions, and then I reached out to a few old friends of mine. Very smart, very well connected friends, and very knowledgeable when it comes to the more obscure security agencies.'

'You shouldn't have done any of this without my authoriza-tion,' said the Professor. 'Who did you talk to?'

'No one you'd know,' said Mike. 'And you're not in charge here! You never were, really. You were just put here to crack the whip and report on us to your bosses. But we've moved beyond that. Our work is over, it's all about survival now.'

'What do you know, Mike?' said Paul. 'What did your contacts tell you?'

'According to my very knowledgeable friends, there's no such thing as the Organization, which Ishmael claims he works for.'

'Of course they wouldn't have heard of us,' I said calmly. 'When you work at our level, none of us exist officially.'

'How very convenient!' said Mike. 'I also had them check your name, and hers. And again they couldn't find any trace of you.'

'Of course not,' I said. 'You didn't really think that "Ishmael Jones" was my real name, did you? Does it even sound real? It's a one-time-use name, for fieldwork. And so is "Penny".'

The Professor sniffed loudly. 'I could have told you that, Mike. If you'd bothered to ask.'

Mike subsided, reluctantly. Not because he was convinced, but because he'd run out of ammunition. For the moment.

Of course his friends couldn't find me. That was part of the deal I made with the Organization. For as long as I worked for them, no matter where I went or what I did, they'd make sure I left no trace in the world. Ishmael Jones is always going to be just a ghost in the machinery. Penny leaned in close to murmur to me.

'There's no official record of me? I don't exist?'

'Relax,' I said. 'Mike's friends would have found you easily enough if they'd looked on the electoral roll and places like that, but that wasn't what they were looking for.'

'Got it,' said Penny.

'They're muttering to each other again!' Mike said loudly. 'What are they saying that we're not allowed to hear?'

The Professor rounded on him. 'Mike, will you please shut up! We're in a very dangerous situation, and you're not helping!' She turned to me. 'Whether we want to admit it or not, I think it's clear it's become too dangerous for us to stay in the camp any longer. Can you get us out of here?'

Penny put a hand on my arm. 'I really think we should go, Ishmael. You wanted to save as many people as you could, and this might be the only way to do it.'

I looked at her steadily. 'You think we should just run away?'

'We didn't come here to solve the mystery of the hole,' she said steadily. 'We were supposed to protect these people. I haven't forgotten what you said earlier, about what the Organization might do to you. But you also said that wasn't important compared to protecting these people. Unless you've changed your mind.'

'No,' I said. 'I haven't. All right, then. If we're going to leave, that means walking down the hillside in the dark to where we parked the car. Is everyone OK with that?'

The three scientists looked at the darkness pressing close to the perimeter. They didn't look too happy, but it wasn't enough to dissuade them.

'Phone the Colonel first, Ishmael,' said Penny. 'Tell him we're leaving, and why. Don't give him a chance to argue, just tell him to send in enough armed men to surround the area, and once we're safely out they can move in and seal off the campsite.'

'Sounds like a plan to me,' I said. I smiled at her. 'You always were the brains in this outfit.'

'I know,' said Penny. She smiled dazzlingly.

'So,' said Paul, as I took my phone out of my pocket, 'we're not waiting for Mr Carroll?'

'You really want to stay here that long?' said Mike.

'At least Carroll works for a Government department,' Paul said patiently. 'As you already pointed out, we don't really know anything about Ishmael, or the Colonel or his Organization.'

'I know the Colonel,' said the Professor. 'I vouch for him.'

Paul shook his head. 'No offence, Professor, but right now that's not enough.'

'The Colonel can send in a small army of armed men right now,' said Penny. 'Long before Black Heir could arrange anything similar.'

'Call your Colonel,' said Mike.

I started to dial the number. Then stopped and looked at my phone.

'What?' Mike said immediately. 'What is it? What's wrong?'

'Have you let your battery go flat again?' said Penny.

'There's no signal,' I said.

I got up and walked around, even holding the phone above my head, but couldn't get a single bar. I shook the phone hard and tried again.

'You know that never works . . .' said Penny.

I nodded, put the phone away, and sat down. 'Either there's no coverage in this area, or the hole is interfering with the signal.'

The scientists looked at each other, and then up the hill at the hole. As though it might be listening.

'We never thought to check whether the hole might be interfering with our communications,' said the Professor.

'Why would we?' said Paul. 'That isn't what we came here for.'

'Why would the hole do that?' said Mike.

'Why does it do anything?' said Paul.

He'd made a bigger point than he realized. I'd accepted that the hole had been affecting my senses, but now I had to wonder what else the hole might be doing to us, and possibly to our surroundings, that we hadn't noticed.

'Have you ever wondered,' Mike said suddenly, 'whether the hole might have been put here specifically to mess with us? To present us with problems to solve, just to see how we cope? All the time we thought we were investigating the hole, it might have been investigating us.'

'You mean, we're its lab rats?' said the Professor. 'That the hole has had us running through a maze we can't even see?'

'That's a horrid thought!' said Penny.

'If the hole is running tests on us,' said Paul, 'I wonder how we're doing . . .'

'I'll try my phone,' said Penny.

She started to reach for it, but I put a hand on her arm. 'You couldn't contact the Colonel, even if I gave you his number. My phone comes with built-in security clearances. Without them, you couldn't even get his phone to ring.'

Penny looked at me. 'You never told me that before.'

'You never asked.'

'We will talk about this later,' Penny said coldly.

'Of course we will,' I said.

'So,' Mike said heavily, 'no reinforcements, after all. Well, that's just great! You get all our hopes up and . . .'

'Mike!' the Professor said sharply. 'Not now!'

'I'm not allowed to speak my mind anymore?' said Mike.

'No,' said the Professor.

Mike looked at her. 'Why not?'

'Because you're being really annoying,' said the Professor.

'I wonder why,' said Mike.

'You mustn't take everything out on Ishmael,' Penny said gently. 'He's not responsible for Ellie's death.'

'He didn't save her,' said Mike.

'He knows that,' said Penny. 'Ishmael takes his job very seriously. But even he can't save everyone.'

'Then what use is he?' said Mike.

Penny's eyes narrowed, but when she answered Mike her voice was cool and composed. 'He's your only hope of getting out of here alive.'

She turned to me. 'We're going to the car. Right now.'

I nodded. 'Because keeping these people safe is why we're here.'

'Exactly,' said Penny.

We all got to our feet. The scientists looked out at the dark,

and I could see a mixture of feelings in their faces. They were
ready enough to leave the camp, but the thought of what might
be waiting for them out in the dark still made them hesitate.
Penny moved in beside me.

'If the Organization does take back its protection and you
have to go on the run, I'm going with you.'

'I can't ask that of you,' I said.

'You don't have to,' she said.

'They're smiling!' said Mike. 'What have they got to smile
about?'

'Shut up, Mike,' I said.

Everyone looked at me expectantly. I think they were hoping
for an encouraging speech, telling them they had nothing to
worry about. But I prefer not to lie to people if I don't have
to, so when in doubt focus on practical things. I looked at the
Professor.

'Do you have a flashlight?'

She frowned. 'There should be one somewhere. I studied
Black Heir's inventory pretty carefully, because I had to sign
for everything. I'm sure it mentioned flashlights.'

'Probably under *To be supplied later*,' growled Mike.

'I will hit you in a minute, Mike,' said the Professor. 'And
it will hurt.'

He looked at her to see if she meant it, and shut up. The
Professor sniffed loudly, and turned back to me.

'If there are any flashlights, they'll be somewhere in the
equipment centre. I'll go and look.'

'No one goes anywhere on their own,' I said. 'We'll go with
you.'

They were all eager to get moving, but I made them wait
a moment while I took a good look round the campsite first.
The open space seemed perfectly still and quiet, the steep
grassy hillside starkly illuminated by the perimeter lights.
Nothing was moving anywhere, and everything seemed as it
should be.

I didn't trust any of it.

'We go straight to the equipment centre,' I said. 'No falling
behind, no side trips, no one going off on their own for any
reason.'

'Or what?' said Mike, rising as always to anything he could take as a challenge.

'Or I'll let the Professor deal with you,' I said.

Mike looked at the Professor, and didn't say anything.

I led the way up the hill to the equipment centre. I didn't need to tell them to stick close together; the silence in the camp and the darkness outside it were enough to convince everyone not to fall behind. There was a certain sense of relief in the group now they were finally doing something. It didn't take long to reach the open structure, and Penny and I stood guard as the three scientists searched through the bits and pieces stacked haphazardly on the shelves. Spare parts, backup pieces, useful items . . . Basically whatever Black Heir thought would come in handy. All of it just dumped on the shelves, for whenever the scientists got around to sorting through them.

The Professor muttered crossly to herself as she picked things up and put them down again. Mike rummaged through the shelves with both hands, swearing quietly and throwing things to the floor when they got in his way. Paul was quiet and methodical, his face as calm and disinterested as ever. I was beginning to wonder what it would take to break a composure like that. Because in my experience when that kind of self-control finally breaks, it's usually sudden and violent. I could feel tension growing in the centre. None of the scientists wanted to walk down the hill in the dark without any light. They shot quick looks through the clear-plastic walls as they worked; as though afraid something might suddenly appear out of nowhere to stop them, now they were so close to escaping. And then the Professor cried out triumphantly, and brandished a heavy military-style flashlight.

'I knew this was here somewhere!'

'Just the one?' said Mike.

'So it would seem,' said the Professor. 'Though I'm sure I saw more than one on the inventory . . .'

'Turn it on,' said Mike. 'Let's make sure the damn thing works before we start celebrating.'

'You don't trust anything, do you?' said Paul.

'Do you?' said Mike.

'I think I used to,' said Paul. 'But recent events have changed my mind.'

The flashlight worked first time, casting a reassuringly bright light. The Professor turned it off again.

'Just preserving the batteries,' she said briskly.

'You really think one flashlight's going to be enough?' said Mike. 'Out there in the night, with no moon or stars? Anything could happen once we leave the camp.'

'Changed your mind about going?' said Paul.

'Not even a little bit,' said Mike. 'I just want us to be safe while we do it.'

'I'm not sure that's an option any more,' said Paul.

'Do you have a better idea?' I asked him.

'No he doesn't and even if he does we're still going,' Mike said flatly. 'And the sooner the better. This isn't a research site any more. It's a killing ground.'

Paul just shrugged, then looked at me. 'How far is it to your car?'

'Just a short walk down the hill,' I said. 'We parked below the archaeological dig.'

'It might be just a short walk in the daylight,' said Mike. 'But in the dark . . .'

'It's not like we're going to get lost along the way,' said Penny. 'All we have to do is keep going down until we reach the dig, and our car is just over the rise beyond that.'

'What if someone's stolen it?' said Mike.

'Mike!' said the Professor.

'What?'

'Mouth is open, should be shut,' said the Professor.

'Couldn't have put it better myself,' I said. 'Let's go.'

'Right now?' said Paul.

'Yes, right now!' said the Professor. 'Can you name one thing here we'll be sorry to leave behind?'

'Give me a moment,' said Paul.

'No more moments,' said the Professor. She hefted the flashlight. 'Lead the way please, Ishmael.'

'Stick behind me, Professor,' I said. 'And shine the light so I can see where we're going. Penny, watch the rear. Mike and

Paul, make sure you stay inside the light. It would be only too easy to get lost in a dark like that.'

'Finally,' Mike growled. 'Something we can agree on.'

We strode back down through the camp, heading for the perimeter and the dark. Everyone stuck so close behind me they were practically treading on my heels. I didn't mind, it meant they'd been paying attention for once. Penny hesitated as we passed the fire.

'Should we put that out? We don't want to risk it spreading to the rest of the site. All it would take is a breath of wind and the flames . . .'

'There hasn't been a breath of wind since we got here,' I said. 'Leave the fire. We might need it if we have to come back.'

'Come back?' Mike said immediately. 'Why the hell would we want to do that? What could possibly go wrong with a short walk down the hill?'

'You've changed your tune!' said the Professor, amused. 'You're usually the pessimist, you tell us.'

'I'm just considering the possibilities,' said Mike.

'Well, don't,' said the Professor.

I led them past the perimeter lights and out of the camp, plunging into the dark without hesitating. Because I didn't want to give the scientists time to think about what they were doing. Leaving the brightly lit camp was like diving into a dark ocean, with no idea whether there might be sharks in the neighbourhood. The Professor's flashlight produced a powerful beam of light, but it didn't penetrate nearly as far into the darkness as I thought it should. Surprisingly for a military flashlight, it was even having trouble producing enough light for all of us to move in.

The darkness pressed in around us, as though trying to force its way in, and the night was disturbingly quiet. The only sound was the crunching of our feet on the grass. It carried loudly on the night, as though warning we were coming.

I couldn't see anything outside the small pool of light we were walking in. There could have been anything at all in the darkness surrounding us. It felt like we were moving through infinite space; an endless dark universe with no light or life anywhere. I glanced back once at the camp, at the circle of light falling away behind us. It made me feel better to know it was still there.

We trudged on down the steep hill, careful to watch our footing. The grass was slick with dew, and the ground rose and fell with worrying unpredictability. But soon enough the archaeological dig appeared before us in the flashlight's beam, and I heard sighs of relief behind me that at least we hadn't lost our way.

'Keep your eyes open,' I said quietly. 'The archaeologists left some trenches around here.'

'How deep could they be?' said Mike.

'Deep enough to ruin your day if you don't watch where you're going,' I said. 'You want to limp the rest of the way on a broken ankle?'

Mike didn't say anything, but after that everyone was very careful where they put their feet. Now they were close to escaping and were putting the madness of the day behind them, they didn't want to spoil their chances. We left the dig behind and moved on into the dark. The unrelieved darkness and the relentless silence were becoming almost unbearably oppressive. As though the dark resented any evidence of life. Even our footsteps were starting to sound muffled, as though the night was soaking up the sound. The light from the Professor's flashlight seemed as strong as ever. I tried not to think about how dark the night would be if the flashlight were to fail and its light went out.

I glanced back at the others to see how they were doing.

The Professor was staring straight ahead, her gaze determinedly following the flashlight's beam. Penny was keeping up a constant surveillance of the night around and behind her, to make sure we weren't being followed or sneaked up on. Mike actually seemed a little more relaxed now we'd committed ourselves to leaving. Paul just strode along, looking nowhere in particular, apparently unbothered as to where we were or where we were going. That was starting to worry me. No one should be that calm. Unless they were deep in shock or denial.

'What if the car isn't there?' Mike said suddenly.

Everyone looked at him.

'Why wouldn't it be there?' said the Professor.

'It's supposed to be parked just beyond the digs,' said Mike. 'But we've been walking for ages and we still haven't reached it.'

'It's the dark,' I said. 'Makes it difficult to judge distances.'

'But what if the car really isn't there?' Mike said stubbornly. 'What would we do then?'

'Mike, you have moved beyond annoying,' said the Professor. 'You are now officially a pain in the arse. So shut the hell up and keep walking, or I will have Ishmael gag you.'

Mike looked at me uncertainly. 'You wouldn't . . .'

'Oh, he would,' said Penny. 'And he'd use a really dirty handkerchief.'

'You're all bullies,' said Mike.

He stumbled along, maintaining a rebellious silence and looking put upon. Everyone else had some kind of smile on their face. Shortly after, there were loud sounds of relief from everyone, as we stumbled over a sudden sharp rise and fall and Penny's Rover appeared in the flashlight's beam. We hurried down the hill towards it, forgetting our usual caution, like passengers on a sinking ship who'd finally spotted a lifeboat.

'Wait a minute,' said Mike, as we drew closer. 'This is your car? This old piece of crap?'

'It's vintage,' Penny said coldly.

Mike sniffed loudly. 'Are we going to need a starting handle to get it going?'

'If I had one I'd insert it in you,' said Penny.

'Don't insult her car,' I said quietly to Mike. 'Really. Don't.'

Penny unlocked the Rover, and we all scrambled inside. Penny settled into place behind the steering wheel, while I took shotgun. The Professor, Mike and Paul crammed themselves into the rear seat. It was a tight fit, shoulder to shoulder and knee to knee, but none of them complained. We were leaving, and that was all that mattered. The Professor made a low relieved sound and turned off her flashlight, happy to bask in the cosy interior light of the car. Penny put her key in the ignition and turned it. Nothing happened. No revving of the engine, not even the slow grinding of a drained battery, just silence. Penny pulled the key out, looked at it, slammed it back in and tried again. Still nothing. It was suddenly horribly quiet inside the car.

'I don't believe it . . .' Mike said despairingly.

I didn't know what to say. Of all the things I'd thought might go wrong and prepared myself for, this wasn't one of them.

'You'd better open the bonnet,' I said to Penny. 'We'll check the engine.'

'There shouldn't be anything wrong with it,' said Penny. 'I had the car serviced only last month.'

She hit the bonnet release, and we all got out of the car. The sound of the doors slamming seemed very loud in the quiet, and the night seemed even darker. The Professor turned her flashlight back on and waved the beam around, just to make sure nothing was taking advantage of the situation. All that showed up in the beam were quick glimpses of open hillside.

'Keep the light on Penny and me, Professor,' I said steadily. 'We need to see what we're doing.'

The Professor nodded quickly, and covered us with the flashlight as we moved around to the front of the car and pushed up the bonnet. Penny and I looked inside, and said nothing. Because we didn't know what to say. Mike stirred impatiently.

'Is it something obvious? Can you fix it?'

'The engine's gone,' said Penny.

'We know that,' said Paul. 'Can you see what the problem is, and what needs doing to fix it?'

'No,' I said. 'It's gone. The engine isn't here.'

The others crowded in around Penny and me, and we all stared into the empty void where the engine should have been. It had been ripped out, leaving nothing but the ends of broken cables and a few scattered bits and pieces. I thought briefly about searching the surrounding area for the engine. But even as I thought that, I knew it wouldn't be possible to get it working again.

'Someone's been busy,' I said finally.

'Look what they've done to my car . . .' said Penny.

'So,' said Paul, his voice surprisingly calm. 'We're not going anywhere.'

'It's been one of those days, hasn't it?' said Mike. He sounded too tired to be angry. 'When did this happen?'

'Could have happened any time after we arrived,' I said.

The Professor struggled to keep her voice steady, though the hand holding the flashlight trembled noticeably. 'Wouldn't we have heard something?'

'We've had a lot of distractions,' I said.

'At least now we can be reasonably sure a Beast isn't behind what's happening,' Penny said steadily. 'An animal wouldn't do something like this.'

'If it's coming out of the hole, it must be something more than just an animal,' said Mike.

'It still wouldn't know what to do with a car, would it?' said Penny. 'It wouldn't do something as specific as this. Taking the engine means human thinking . . . and human mischief.'

'Someone doesn't want us to leave,' I said.

'We got that!' said Mike.

'Could a human being do this?' said Paul.

'If motivated enough,' I said.

'Well,' said Paul, 'you learn something new every day.'

'Is this supposed to reassure us?' said Mike. 'That our unknown killer is only human?'

'A human killer has to be a lot less dangerous than some legendary Beast or an invading alien,' I said.

'Really?' said Paul. 'You don't think someone who could do something like this would be more than usually dangerous?'

Mike glared at him. 'Why are you taking all of this so bloody calmly?'

'Getting excited won't help,' said Paul.

'But if a human being did this,' said the Professor, 'that means the killer has to be one of us. Doesn't it?'

I'd been hoping none of them would make that particular connection just yet. I needed the scientists to cooperate, until I could work out how to deal with this mess. But now they were all glaring at each other suspiciously, as though seeing their companions clearly for the first time.

'What do we do now?' Mike said finally.

'The car's no use,' said the Professor. 'But we could still make our way down the hill until we reach the road. Then follow that till we hit the nearest town. I know it's a long way, but at least we could then find a hotel and phone the police for help.'

'The Colonel wouldn't like that,' I said.

'Screw the Colonel!' said Mike. 'A hotel means light and warmth and good solid walls to put between us and the night. Ellie was always a great believer in walls.'

'But it's still a long way down the hill to the main road,' I said. 'In the dark. No lights, remember? How far do you think we'd get?'

Mike looked like he wanted to argue, but couldn't find the words. He shrugged angrily.

'Do what you want. You will anyway.'

'What do you think we should do, Ishmael?' said Penny.

'Go back to the campsite,' I said steadily. 'Stay by the fire, wait out the night, and talk to Mr Carroll when he makes his call. He can send in people to secure the area, and transport to take us out of here.'

'That's it?' said Mike. 'That's all you've got to offer?'

'It can't be long till the dawn now,' I said. 'Things will seem a lot better once it's light.'

'Are you sure of that?' said Paul.

'Of course,' I said.

I couldn't tell them that I needed to keep everyone together because I couldn't let any of them leave. Not when one of them could be the murderer.

'I really thought we were free of the camp,' said the Professor.

'I don't want to go back,' Mike said quietly. 'I hate it. It's awful there.'

He didn't want to go back to the place where Ellie was murdered. Where her body was.

'We have to go back,' said Paul. 'Because there's nowhere else to go.'

'And we need to go now,' said Penny. 'While the flashlight is still working.'

'Just when you think things can't get any worse . . .' said Mike.

We strode back up the hill a lot faster than we'd gone down it, despite the steep slope. The thought that someone had deliberately stopped us from leaving weighed heavily on our minds. Because that could only mean our mystery killer wasn't finished with us yet. It did help that we could see the brightly lit camp up ahead, shining like a beacon in the dark. The camp might not be safe, but at least it was familiar. And somewhere where we could be sure of seeing who was coming for us. But as the camp drew nearer, I couldn't help wondering if when we got there we'd find someone waiting for us. Someone we'd never even suspected, waiting and smiling, with death in his eyes and in his hands.

I made sure I was the first to cross the perimeter into the camp, ready to fight if need be. But there was nobody there. The whole setting was open and empty, and just as quiet as before. The fire was still burning, so I led everyone over to it, and they all dropped down in their usual places. They found the fire wonderfully warm after the cold on the side of the hill. They'd all been too busy to notice at the time, but now we were back everyone was shaking and shivering. I joined in, even though I don't feel the cold; because I prefer not to stand out. There was an air of exhaustion around the fire, of people driven beyond their physical and emotional limits. Which was bad, because really tired people have a tendency to make really bad decisions.

'At least the fire didn't go out,' Penny said finally.

'It is something of a comfort,' said the Professor.

'But not much,' said Mike.

'I'd hit you, if I had the energy,' said the Professor.

'Just as well you don't . . .' said Mike.

They managed a small smile for each other. Paul had gone back to looking out at the dark. Perhaps he thought that was where the next threat would come from, and he didn't want to miss it. I wasn't sure any of the scientists realized just how dangerous the situation was now. The killer had us trapped; in a place he or she knew well, with no way out. I looked at Penny.

'I'm sorry about your car. I know you were fond of it.'

'I liked it because it was such a workhorse,' said Penny. 'Always kept going, never complained . . . When I saw the engine was gone, it felt like someone ripped the heart out of my favourite pet.'

Mike started to say something, caught the look in my eye, and thought better of it.

'You can always buy another Rover, once we get back,' I said to Penny.

'It wouldn't be the same.' She managed a smile for me. 'You've never understood about people and their cars.'

'People are strange,' I said solemnly.

We all sat quietly together for a while, lost in our own thoughts. I was trying to think of something, anything, I could do to keep these people safe. Slowly it became clear to me that I did have one other option: I could leave the scientists here, with Penny, and go off on my own. If I went down the hill without them, I could make much better speed; and I'd back myself against anything I might meet along the way. Once I got to the nearest town, I could contact the Colonel and make him send in reinforcements. Then I could hurry back up the hill to the camp and reassure everyone that help was on its way.

Except . . . I couldn't leave Penny here, with these people. Not when one of them could be a cold-blooded killer. I'd trust Penny to look after herself under most circumstances; but these weren't most circumstances. And . . . I had a horrible feeling that if I did leave, I might return to find everyone sitting around the fire with their heads missing. Or maybe find every single one of them had vanished. Nothing left in the camp, apart from the hole.

So, I wasn't going anywhere.

I thought about the missing car engine. There had been something calculating about that, as though the killer was playing with us. Why not just trash the car? Slash the tyres, set it on fire, wreck it? Because then whoever did it wouldn't have been able to enjoy watching the rest of us have our moment of relief, of feeling safe at last because we thought we were getting away. Leaving us to discover that the engine was missing, and we weren't going anywhere after all, was crueller. And that thought made me see the deaths of Robert and Ellie in a whole new light. I'd been assuming the way they died was down to simple expediency: using the edge of the hole as a weapon because it was all the killer had. But what if they were killed in such a disturbing way deliberately? What if the killer had set out to terrorize everyone? Or maybe just thought it was funny . . .

I really didn't like the way my thoughts were going.

Mike looked at the tent that held the dead bodies. 'It feels wrong, dumping Ellie in there with Robert and Terry. She should be in her own tent.'

'Ellie isn't really in there,' I said, as kindly as I could. 'Just what she left behind. Like her clothes.'

'Is that supposed to reassure me?' said Mike.

'I don't know,' I said. 'Maybe.'

He stopped for a moment, and then smiled briefly as he recognized his own words from earlier. He nodded, acknowledging the point.

'Do you want me to move Ellie?' I said. 'I will if that would help.'

Mike thought about it, then shook his head. 'No, you're right. It wouldn't make any difference.'

'Do you believe in ghosts?' said the Professor.

We all looked at her. She seemed quite serious.

'Where did that come from?' said Mike. Then he stopped and looked at her sharply. 'Have you been seeing things?'

'It's just that I wonder, sometimes,' said the Professor. 'Whether we're haunted by the ghosts of all the people we've hurt.'

'That sounds more like conscience than ghosts,' Penny said carefully.

'I never look back,' said Paul. 'Only forward.'

'Yes, well, that's because you're young,' said the Professor.

'And weird,' said Mike.

No one seemed to have anything to say after that, so we just sat quietly round the fire. Looking at the flames and the camp and the dark, so we wouldn't have to look at each other and wonder if we were looking into the face of a killer. But if one of us was responsible for the death of three people, why wasn't the killer doing anything? Why not split us up? Get us to go off on our own so we'd be easier targets? Or was the killer just enjoying the moment? Savouring our fear, laughing inside as we sat there helplessly without a clue.

'It's very dark, out there,' Paul said finally. Since we returned to the camp, he hadn't taken his eyes off the night. 'We're so far from civilization there's not a light to be seen anywhere.'

'There should be some,' said the Professor, frowning. 'Nearby towns, farmhouses . . . And we should be able to see Bath on the horizon.'

'There's still no moon or stars,' said Mark, frowning at the endless dark overhead. 'What's happened to them?'

'Low cloud cover,' said the Professor.

'Yeah, right,' said Mike.

'It makes you wonder if there's anything left out there,' said Paul, his voice eerily calm. 'If the world has just gone away, or the dark has eaten everything up . . . If we're all that's left now, alone in the night.'

'Don't!' said Penny, shuddering. 'You are really creeping me out, Paul.'

'Yeah,' said Mike. 'What kind of talk is that for a scientist?'

'We have enough problems as it is, without bringing existential dread into it,' said the Professor.

'But then why can't we see anything? Or hear anything?' Paul finally turned his eyes away from the dark to look at each of us in turn. His face was calm, and his voice sounded entirely reasonable. 'Doesn't it feel like we've been deliberately isolated, cut off from everything? As if the hole sucked in everything else, so it wouldn't have to share us.'

'Cut the crap!' Mike said roughly. 'The missing car engine is all the proof we needed that the killer isn't any Beast, or some alien thing. The killer is one of us. Sitting right here, playing mind games and laughing up their sleeve at the rest of us.' He turned abruptly to look at me. 'And I'll say it again, no one started dying until you turned up.'

'Haven't we already been through this?' I said calmly.

'We didn't finish because I got shouted down,' said Mike. 'There's still things we need to talk about.'

'Like what?' said the Professor.

'Like we still can't be sure he is who he claims to be,' Mike said stubbornly. 'Or even why he's here.'

'We were sent by the Colonel to protect you,' said Penny. 'What else do you need to know?'

'We're supposed to just take your word for that?' said Mike.

'What else can you do?' I said calmly. 'You need us if you want to stay alive.'

'Ishmael!' Penny said quickly. 'Sorry, everyone. He's not really a people person. But think about it. If we're not who we say we are, how did we know where to find you? How could we have known about the hole if the Colonel hadn't briefed us?'

The scientists considered that, but none of them seemed particularly convinced.

'You could be spies,' said Mike. 'Secret agents in the service of some foreign power, here to steal our secrets.'

'What secrets?' said the Professor. 'We haven't discovered anything worth stealing. And they couldn't steal the hole if they tried.'

'I think proper secret agents would have been a bit more professional in their approach,' said Paul. 'Not made such a mess of things. And people.'

Mike glared at him. 'Now who's having problems with their people skills?'

'We can either assume Ishmael and Penny are who they say they are and feel protected,' Paul said reasonably, 'or distrust them and feel in danger of our lives . . . Since we don't have any evidence one way or the other, it all comes down to personal choice. We either pick something that makes us feel safer, or something that makes us feel threatened.'

'He's right, Mike,' the Professor said steadily. 'We have to trust Ishmael and Penny, because they're the only ones with the skills and experience to get us through this night alive.'

'But three people are dead!' said Mike. 'Four, if you count the archaeologist.'

'All of those people died because they got too close to the hole,' I said. 'We know better.'

'Right,' said Penny, pulling a face. 'I wouldn't go near that thing again if you put a gun to my head.'

Mike shook his head. 'There's nothing you can say that will make me feel safe. The killer's been one step ahead of us all the way.'

'Where are you going with this, Mike?' said the Professor.

'The only people I could be sure of were Ellie and Robert,' said Mike. 'Because I knew them from before. And they're both dead now. So any one of you could be some kind of ringer, a spy, or an assassin sent to shut down the operation. I think I should go back to my computer and have my devious little friends dig into everyone's background.'

'This is no time for paranoia,' said the Professor.

'It's not paranoia when someone really is trying to kill you!' said Mike.

Paul stood up suddenly and stared out into the dark. His face was set in harsh lines, his voice cold and flat.

'Someone's out there.'

We were all up and on our feet in a moment, looking where he was looking, staring past the perimeter lights into a darkness without end. We might as well have been looking at a blank wall. The night was very quiet, and very still. As if it was watching us.

'Everyone make a circle, with their backs to the fire!' I said, keeping my voice carefully calm and controlled. 'We need to be looking in all directions at once. We don't want anything sneaking up on us from behind because we're all looking at where it used to be.'

Everyone moved quickly to form a circle, staring out into the dark in every direction at once. I could feel the tension rising among them. Mike was eager to confront something, so he could strike out at it, punish it for what it had done. Penny was readying herself for action, a dependable presence. The Professor was so tightly strung she could barely get her breath. Only Paul appeared unaffected by the general atmosphere, staring unwaveringly out into the dark.

'Is this night never going to end?' said Mike.

'Not now, Mike,' I said. 'What did you see, Paul?'

'I didn't see anything.' Paul's voice was entirely steady. 'I heard something. Movements, perhaps footsteps. Out there, in the night.'

'Human footsteps?' said the Professor.

'I don't know,' said Paul.

I scowled. I hadn't heard anything. And I should have, if there was something moving around in the darkness. Had the hole really shut down my senses that much? I concentrated. I could smell Penny's familiar perfume, but not the scents of the others. I could hear all of them moving, the rustle of their clothes as they shifted their weight uncertainly, but not their heartbeats. I glared out into the night. Nothing was moving out there; I would have heard something, sensed something. I was sure of that. Except I couldn't be sure of anything anymore.

I glanced round at the others. The Professor was trembling in all her limbs now, staring wildly about her. The lines in her face had deepened under the pressure of stress and dread, and her eyes looked oddly lost; as if she couldn't understand what was happening. Mike was so tense he was actually quivering like a greyhound in a trap; desperate to unleash his anger and frustration on whatever was out there. His hands had clenched into fists again, and his mouth was a flat grim line. Paul just stared out into the darkness, as though he couldn't look away because he was expecting something to emerge from the night and stare back at him. Had he really heard something? Or was he finally cracking up? Penny stood tall and steady, ready for anything. Because she was never scared of anything when there were people who needed protecting.

I turned back to look at the darkness in front of me. I've never liked the dark; because it hides things from me.

'Come on, you bastard!' Mike yelled suddenly. 'Come into the light, so we can see you! I'm not scared of you! Come forward and face me, so I can beat the shit out of you! You cowardly little turd!'

'Probably not a good idea to taunt the unknown homicidal maniac,' murmured Paul. 'Or the unknown killer Beast.'

Mike tore his eyes away from the dark just long enough to glare at Paul. 'There isn't any Beast! Our killer is a human being. Has to be.'

'Perhaps sometimes it's human, and sometimes a Beast,' said Paul.

Everyone turned to look at him. Because this was a new thought.

'A werewolf?' said Mike. 'Seriously?'

Penny and I exchanged a look. We'd fought a shapeshifter on one of our previous cases. A devious creature that hid among the very people it was preying on. Why hadn't I thought of that? Mike saw the look pass between Penny and me, and was immediately suspicious.

'What do you know about werewolves?'

'Shapeshifters are always hard to deal with,' I said. 'Beasts that hide within people. Coming out to kill and then disappearing back into the perfect hiding place.'

'Werewolves are real?' said the Professor, her voice rising.

'Sometimes,' said Penny.

'And unfortunately I didn't think to bring a silver dagger,' I said. 'Anyone else have one? No? I didn't think so.'

'I have a silver crucifix,' said Mike, unexpectedly.

'Not terribly useful for stabbing people,' I said.

'Does it have to be silver?' said the Professor.

'Not always,' I said. 'But silver is usually the way to bet.'

'Ishmael and I heard something moving around in the dark outside the camp earlier tonight,' said Penny.

'It's the Beast,' said Paul, serenely. 'Something that came up out of the hole to run wild in the world. I think it got tired of waiting for us to go to it, so now it's come looking for us.'

'OK . . .' said Mike. 'Someone has lost the plot, big time.'

'Shut up, Mike!' said the Professor.

'Are we really taking the idea of werewolves seriously?' said Mike. 'They're just . . . ancient legends and in old movies. We're scientists!'

'I'm so scared I'm ready to believe in anything,' said the Professor. 'And it would explain a lot, wouldn't it? That's why parts of the bodies were missing. The Beast took them away to eat later.'

'And if the Beast is out there now,' I said, 'that means the killer isn't one of us, after all.'

'Unless someone in the tent wasn't as dead as we thought,' said Paul.

We all looked across at the tent that held Terry, Robert and Ellie. The flaps still seemed securely closed.

'But . . . why would something as powerful as a werewolf need to hide in the dark?' said Penny.

'Maybe it's playing with us,' said Paul. 'Maybe to the Beast it's all fun and games . . .'

'Hold it, hold it!' said Mike. 'What do we think this is now? A human that turns into a wolf when the moon is full? Except we haven't got a moon. Or a Beast from the other side of the hole?'

'I don't know!' the Professor said sharply. 'Why don't you go out into the dark and ask it?'

'Maybe it's already got into the camp,' said Paul.

'Am I the only one who winces every time he says anything?' said Mike.

'Keep looking and keep listening,' I said sharply. 'Watch the camp as well as the night. Make sure whatever it is isn't sneaking up on us.'

'We can't just stand here for ever,' said Mike.

'Hush!' said Penny. 'Don't make any noise it could hide behind. And let Ishmael think, so he can come up with something.'

We all stood very still, in our circle round the fire, straining our senses against our surroundings. I could hear the crackling of the flames and everyone else's hurried breathing, but nothing to suggest anything was moving anywhere in the camp or out in the dark. I'd reached the point where I wanted something to appear so I could be sure what it was we were facing. So I'd have some idea what to do.

'I'm not hearing anything moving,' Penny said finally. 'Can any of you hear anything?'

Mike and the Professor shook their heads. Paul was still staring fixedly out into the night. I could feel the others start to relax, as they began to believe whatever had been out there had come and gone. Penny looked at me hopefully, but all I could do was shrug.

'Paul,' I said. 'I think we can stand down now.'

'No,' he said. 'This isn't over yet.'

'Paul . . .'

'The danger isn't over.'

'Can you at least point to where you heard the sounds?' I said.

'Of course.'

He pointed out into the darkness, with a very steady arm. And while everyone's attention was fixed on that direction, Paul grabbed hold of Penny, picking her up bodily under one arm, and ran off with her up the hill to the hole. Penny fought him fiercely, but couldn't break his grip. Paul carried her easily, as though she was weightless. I yelled to the Professor and Mike to stay put, and sprinted after Paul. He was moving inhumanly quickly, but so was I. He got to the hole first, slammed to a halt in front of it, and turned to face me, still holding Penny. I crashed to a halt, facing him. Neither of us was breathing hard.

Paul smiled easily at me. Penny fought him with everything she had, but still couldn't break free. Paul ignored her efforts, all his attention fixed on me. I took a step forward, and then stopped abruptly as Paul closed his free hand around Penny's throat. She stopped struggling, and he released his hold just enough for her to breathe again. I nodded to Penny reassuringly, and she managed a smile for me.

I was standing on one side of the safety line, and Paul was on the other. Far too close to the hole and its razor-sharp edges for my liking.

'So,' he said easily. 'Here we are, at last. No more fun and games. Time for the truth at last.'

'What's going on, Paul?' I said. 'What's happening here?'

'I just got tired of playing,' he said. 'It's time to cut to the chase. Time to do what I came here to do.'

'Don't do anything foolish, Paul,' I said.

His smiled widened.

'I'm not Paul.'

He turned and jumped into the hole, taking Penny with him, and they both disappeared into the bottomless dark.

FIVE

Conversation on a Beach that Isn't a Beach

I jumped into the hole after them.

It was like diving into pitch-black waters, a night-dark ocean with no end to it. I had a moment to remember the look on Terry's face, after we hauled his dead body out of the hole. The look of absolute horror, the features twisted and distorted from seeing something so unbearable he had to die to get away from it. But I was willing to bet I'd seen a lot more of the horrors of the world than he had. Whatever was at the bottom of the hole, I was ready to face it.

For Penny.

Just like before, all light disappeared the moment I entered the hole. I couldn't see anything, not even the coloured flecks you sometimes get when you close your eyes in a darkened room. I couldn't hear anything either; not even my own breathing or heartbeat. I might have been anywhere, or nowhere. I tried to touch my face with my hands, just to reassure myself I still existed, but I couldn't seem to find my hands. Couldn't even tell where they were in relation to my body. I wasn't sure whether I was falling down or up, or even where up and down might be. And there was no cable attached to the back of my belt to get me home again.

I was falling, all alone in the dark.

The usual reaction to being trapped somewhere dark is claustrophobia, a feeling of unseen walls closing in on you. I felt the opposite: that I was dropping helplessly through infinite space. Through a universe full of nothing where all the stars had gone out. Just me, and a night without end.

Total sensory deprivation. Only my mind was still working. I reminded myself that some people did this sort of thing for fun. Sealing themselves off from all the intrusive noise and chaos of the world in special sensory-deprivation tanks. I could handle this as long as I concentrated on what mattered: catching up with Paul and Penny and getting her back safely. Then teaching Paul the error of his ways, with stern words and extreme violence.

It helped to know this darkness couldn't go on for ever. Paul, or whoever he really was, had to be going somewhere with Penny. Had to have some destination in mind. An end to all this falling. I remembered the steel cable unwinding from the drum as it disappeared into the hole. It never did get to the bottom. So I had to wonder, just how far down did the hole go?

I made myself be patient. I'd faced much scarier things than the dark, in my time.

The first sensation I felt was of falling through cobwebs. I could feel them brushing against my face; delicate gossamer touches like the fingertips of hesitant ghosts. The thought of unseen cobwebs raised the idea of unseen spiders, with no way of knowing how big they were or how close they might be. They could be all around me, hanging silently in massive webs, watching with clusters of inhuman eyes that could pierce the darkness. Fortunately, I don't share most people's irrational fear of spiders; big or small. I never did understand that. If any spider in here chose to mess with me, I would happily punch it in the head until it gave up on the idea. Always assuming I could find its head. Or my fist.

I tried to grab hold of the cobwebs, not to slow my fall but just to make sure of what it was I was feeling. But I couldn't seem to grasp anything. I was starting to get a feeling of where my hands were in relation to my body; and a sense of movement, of heading towards something. I wondered how fast I was falling, and how hard I would hit when I finally reached the bottom. And yet above all I was fascinated by a sense of familiarity: as if I had been here before. Or if not me, then perhaps whoever I used to be, before I was me.

I fell on, into the dark. I couldn't feel the cobwebs any more, and I was actually starting to feel a bit bored. If all this darkness and distance was supposed to scare or disorientate me, it wasn't working.

I still wasn't getting any real sense of speed or how much
distance I'd covered, or how much further I still had to travel.
But I was definitely approaching somewhere. I could feel it.
Like some people can never get lost, or always know where
the North Star is, I have always been able to feel the world
beneath my feet and know my place on it. I lost that certainty
the moment I entered the hole, but now I could sense a new
world up ahead. Waiting for me. Ellie had been right all along:
the hole wasn't just a hole, but a tunnel connecting one place
with another. Another world, another dimension or reality . . .
Could I even hope to survive in this new place?

The odds favoured it. Paul must have believed he would be
safe there, or he wouldn't have been so ready to jump into
the hole. He hadn't looked like a man intent on suicide. His
smile had been openly mocking; challenging me to come after
him, and Penny. He had all the answers. And I was determined
to get them out of him, one way or another. Once I'd got
Penny away from him safely. I smiled briefly. She was going
to be mad as hell at having to be rescued. I strained my eyes
against the dark, but I still couldn't see any trace of Paul and
Penny falling ahead of me. There was nothing to be seen
anywhere, in this darkness between the worlds.

I had time to wonder why Paul had done all this. And who
he was, if he wasn't really Paul. A spy, a ringer, from some
other secret group? Some inhuman shape-changing thing, from
out of the hole . . .? I thought hard, trying to remember if
there had been any signs or warnings I should have picked
up, any clue that there was something different about Paul. I
didn't think so. He'd always been the quiet one in the group,
the one who seemed to go out of his way not to stand out. To
avoid making the least impression. Was that because he didn't
want to give away that he wasn't the real Paul? Could that be
why he didn't seem as upset as the others when he saw what
had happened to Terry? And then Robert and Ellie?

Could he be responsible for all of the deaths? Had he been
secretly protecting the hole all this time?

I remembered Mike saying we had no way of proving that
any of us were who we claimed to be. He had threatened to
go back to his computers and run background checks on all

of us . . . And that was when Paul distracted us by pretending to hear movements out in the darkness beyond the perimeter lights. Had Mike's threat been enough to finally drive Paul to direct action? But then why kidnap Penny rather than any of the others? Because Paul knew she was the one hostage that would force me to go after him. But why would he want that? What made me so important to the man who wasn't Paul?

There was a sudden blast of light and sound, blinding and dazzling. All my senses were suddenly back and working overtime, filling my head like a crowd of people all shouting at once. When the clamour finally died down to manageable levels, I realized I was standing on my feet, perfectly steadily. Somewhere else I had arrived without any sudden stop or impact. I looked slowly around me. And to my surprise, and even shock, I found I recognized my new setting. I had seen this place before in glimpses: in my dreams, and scraps of memory. This was my old world. Where I originally came from; where I began before I was me.

It looked alien, and strange beyond bearing.

I was standing on a beach made up of stones that shone like diamonds. They were all moving slowly, churning and seething, swirling in complex patterns; as if they were dreaming and stirring in their sleep. The ocean before me was a deep rich purple, its mountainous waves rising up and up like skyscrapers, only to fall slowly back, taking their time; more like some impossibly thick syrup than water. The heavy waves pounded the shore like close-up thunder. Strange lights detonated in the depths, flaring up and then gone in a moment, like phosphorescent stars. I could see huge shapes moving in the languorous ocean, distorted things with hides like diseased metal. I could make out just enough of them to be grateful I couldn't see more. They looked like the kind of things that pursue us in the kind of nightmares we are grateful to wake from.

I looked behind me. There was no sign anywhere of the hole that had brought me here. Just a massive cliff face. A sickly grey surface shot through with dark pulsing veins, it bulged out here and there in smooth almost organic shapes. They reminded me of rotting fruit or fruiting bodies. On top of the cliff I could just make out a huge artificial structure composed of brightly shining metal plates, interrupted by jutting spikes and unnatural projections that came and went in constant motion as the whole structure cycled through endless strange iterations.

And all of this against a bottle-green sky, under a fierce white sun. Three small moons, wrinkled like evil faces, shot across the cloudless sky as if chasing each other in some desperate race for survival. Somehow, I knew they were alive and hungry.

I realized I was instinctively holding my breath and made myself let it out, then I drew in a slow steady breath and relaxed a little as the air turned out to be breathable. It was thick with heavy scents, like poisoned meats and rotting metals, burned bones and the perfumes of corrupt flowers.

There was a sound to my right: the very familiar sound of someone clearing their throat politely. I looked round sharply, and there was Paul; standing not far away, down the beach. I was positive he hadn't been there just a moment before. He was standing quite casually, entirely at his ease in this alien setting. He smiled at me cheerfully; as if I was an expected guest who'd finally shown up for a party. I didn't smile back.

Penny was lying unconscious at Paul's feet. Breathing steadily, eyes closed, her face calm and apparently unaffected by her experience in passing through the hole. That was a relief, after what had happened to Terry. I wondered if he'd been here and seen this world; or something that lived in it. Perhaps this world showed him something it was holding back from me, for now. I started towards Paul, but he stopped me with a raised hand.

'No closer, Ishmael. Penny's fine. And she'll stay that way as long as you keep your distance. Let's both be civilized about this, until we've had our little chat. I knew the transition would be too much for her, so I shut her mind down when we entered the hole, to protect her. You see the circle in the beach, surrounding us? That line marks the boundary of the Earth-style conditions I'm maintaining. Because she wouldn't survive the local conditions for one moment. And neither would you, in that body.' He stopped and looked down at himself, seeming both amused and contemptuous. 'I don't know how you can stand living in something so small. And only five senses? How do you keep from bumping into things?'

'Who are you?' I said.

'I would have thought that was obvious,' he said, still smiling his easy smile. 'I'm an alien passing for human, just like you. Except I'm not a castaway or beachcomber. I was made human and sent to Earth through the hole to find out what happened to your starship. It's been missing for some time now, and we wanted to know why it never reported in.'

'You made the hole?' I said.

'Hardly. We just took advantage of a recurring phenomenon. They do make for such wonderful shortcuts.'

'A tunnel between the worlds . . .' I said.

'Must you take things so literally?' said Paul, a pained look on his face. 'There was a time you understood such things better than I do. But then you've forgotten so much, haven't you?'

'How did you find me?' I said. I was still measuring the distance between Penny and me, trying to work out whether I could get to her before Paul could stop me. But every time I so much as tensed a muscle, he caught my eye and I had to stop.

'You weren't exactly difficult to find,' said Paul. 'Even in that body, you stand out for those who know what to look for. But you'd been gone so long, been human for so long, it was decided I should approach you cautiously. We weren't exactly sure what your reaction might be.'

'What happened to the real Paul?'

'He's gone. It's not like he had much personality. I doubt anyone will miss him. We just took him out of the world and inserted me into what was happening. To look you over, and decide how best to make contact.'

'When did you replace Paul?' I said. 'After he arrived at the campsite, or before? Did I ever meet the real Paul?'

'You can work that out for yourself later,' said Paul, entirely unmoved by the anger in my voice. 'It doesn't matter. Let's move on, and talk about the things that do matter. Starting with what happened to you.'

'The ship crashed,' I said. 'I think something attacked us. The ship fell to Earth like a shooting star, screaming all the way down. And when it hit, it hit hard. The ship was badly damaged, which is probably why it never sent out a distress signal. The rest of the crew died on impact. The transformation machines made me human so I could survive on Earth. But the machines had been damaged in the crash, and they wiped all my memories. Of who and what I was, before I was me. I don't even remember where the ship buried itself.'

'Shame,' said Paul. 'Still, not to worry. I'm sure we'll find it eventually. What matters is that we found you. Your ordeal is finally over. You can come home now.'

'I *was* home,' I said.

He looked at me for a long moment. He seemed honestly shocked.

'You can't mean that . . . You don't belong there! On that awful place! I don't know how you were able to stand it so long. I was only there a short while, to rescue you, and I was going out of my mind with frustration.'

'It's all I've ever known,' I said. 'And it's all I want to know. I made a life for myself on Earth. I belong there now.'

'No you don't,' Paul said sternly. 'This is that body talking, not you. It's time for you to stop slumming, come home, and take up your responsibilities.'

'My only responsibility is to Penny,' I said.

'Forget her! She doesn't matter. It's vitally important that you stop this nonsense and come back to us!'

'Why?' I said.

'You really have forgotten everything, haven't you?'

'Why did you bring Penny here?' I said.

'To make sure you'd follow me,' said Paul. 'I could see you'd been human for so long that you were lost in it, and realized what she meant to you. I kept expecting you to recognize who I was, and gave you every opportunity. But when it became clear you honestly didn't have a clue, I had no choice but to do something dramatic to ensure you'd have no choice but to follow me home.'

'You could have grabbed Penny at any time,' I said. 'It couldn't have taken you long to realize I didn't know you.

But you didn't . . . Because you were having fun, playing games with us.'

'Maybe,' said Paul. 'Just for a while. You must admit, the thing with the car engine was hilarious. But none of that matters. You're home now. Don't concern yourself over Penny. Once we've changed you back to who you really are, you won't care about her any more. I can always dispose of the body for you.'

I took a step forward, and Paul's voice broke off as he took in the look on my face. When I spoke, my voice sounded dangerously cold. Even to me.

'Touch her and I'll kill you.'

For the first time, Paul seemed honestly taken aback. He had to struggle to find the right words.

'You'd attack one of your own kind, over one of them?'

'Her life is more important to me than my own,' I said. 'I'd fight for her. I'd die for her.'

Paul smiled suddenly. 'You really have gone native, haven't you?'

'You could have killed Penny the moment you arrived in this place,' I said. 'Just by exposing her to the local conditions. But instead, you kept her safe till I got here. Because you knew that if you let her die, you'd no longer have any hold over me. And I would be your enemy till the day I die.

'You could have just grabbed me and jumped into the hole, but I don't think you were allowed to do that. All this time you've been talking, trying to persuade me, instead of just turning me back into what I used to be. You can't make me do anything, can you? You need to convince me to do this of my own free will . . . Why? What makes me so important that you went to all this trouble to come after the single survivor of a crashed starship on a backwater world?'

'You're right,' said Paul. 'I can't force you to come home. But I'm not allowed to tell you why. You have no idea how frustrating all of this is. Can't you just trust me? You used to. Would I really have gone to all this effort if your return wasn't so important?'

'Important to you,' I said. 'Not to me.'

Paul sighed dramatically. 'Oh, very well . . . If you're

determined not to listen to reason, then we'll just have to do this the hard way. Take Penny and go back to your little world. She's yours, for as long as she lasts. We can wait. Let her live out her small human life, and when it's over we'll talk again. You and I have golden blood, we walk in eternity. And when you no longer have her to tie you to that pitiful place, we'll come and find you again and bring you home. Back to where you belong.'

'Tell me,' I said. 'Why did the starship go to Earth? If it's such an unimportant place? What was I supposed to do there?'

'Sorry,' said Paul. 'No clues. You wouldn't understand anyway, with your limited human thinking.'

'There's a war going on among the stars, isn't there?'

He looked at me curiously. 'You remember that?'

'I learned that,' I said.

Paul looked at me expectantly, wanting to know who could have told me. But I just smiled back at him. It pleased me, to know something he didn't.

'I suppose you could call it a war,' Paul said finally. 'That's part of why we went to such trouble to find you. Please, come home. You're needed. I could send Penny back safely. Just say the word and you can be restored to your proper self. Then you'll remember everything, and it will all make sense to you.'

'I think . . . that would be like dying,' I said. 'And I'm not ready to do that, just yet.'

Paul shrugged. A surprisingly human gesture in such an inhuman setting. 'Then I'll be off.'

He turned to leave.

'Wait!' I said. 'Why did you kill all those people? Were you just playing games because you were bored?'

He looked back at me, as though I was being very slow. 'I didn't kill anyone. I was only there for you.'

He stepped across the circle's boundary line, and immediately became something else. A shape so alien I had to turn my head away, rather than look at it directly. The new shape sprouted wide membranous wings and flew away, flapping unhurriedly across the purple sea into the green heavens.

I didn't even try to follow where it was going. Just the shape made my head hurt. I ran forward across the shifting stones to kneel beside Penny. She was still breathing steadily, her eyes still closed. I didn't try to wake her. I didn't want her to see any of this, and think of what it meant to the thing I was before I was Ishmael Jones.

I felt a sudden presence behind me. I looked round. And there was the hole, set into the cliff face. The same flat circle, full of an impenetrable darkness, that seemed only to tunnel deep into the cliff. I was relieved to see it, not just because it was our way home but because it was the only truly familiar sight in this alien setting. I suddenly realized that the circle surrounding Penny and me was moving steadily forward, as the Earth conditions shut themselves down. I picked up Penny, and took one last look at the alien world. To my relief, I wasn't at all tempted to stay. Paul was wrong, I didn't belong here. I belonged with Penny.

I held her tightly to me, and jumped back into the hole.

SIX
All Kinds of Mercy

I travelled a lot faster on my return than on my way in. There was no sense of motion, though I was conscious that we were travelling. The same way I could feel Penny in my arms, pressed tight against my chest. The darkness was just as complete as before, but I had no doubt we were making fast progress through it. As if the dark between the worlds couldn't wait to be rid of me.

At least there weren't any cobwebs this time.

It came as something of a surprise when I sensed another presence in the dark with us. Close enough that when it spoke to me I could hear its voice quite distinctly. The Voice sounded cool and calm, but it had an artificial precision that suggested Human wasn't its usual language.

'You are not what you seem,' said the Voice. Not an accusation, more just . . . interested.

'I'm exactly what I seem,' I said politely. 'It's just that I'm something else as well.'

'Something we know, and recognize.'

'Well,' I said, 'that's nice for you.'

'Not really,' said the Voice. 'Why are you here?'

'Just passing through,' I said.

'Travelling to Earth.'

'Yes,' I said. 'Given that both of us are currently inside a hole that has been used to spy on the Earth and its people, would I be correct in assuming you're the ones responsible for doing that?'

'Yes,' said the Voice. 'We've been watching Humanity for some time, observing them as they grew and developed.'

'You really need to stop that,' I said, doing my best to sound firm and severe. 'Leave the Earth alone. It's protected.'

I carefully didn't add anything more to that statement. I

thought it would be more impressive if the Voice didn't know I was the only one protecting all of Humanity.

'We do it because it is necessary,' said the Voice. 'We watch the humans because we are afraid of them. We have seen what they do to each other, and we are concerned that they will find a way to come where we are and do these things to us.'

'If you shut down the holes, they won't be able to get to you,' I said carefully. 'They lack the technology to produce such things themselves. Right now they have no idea you exist, so without the spy holes they'd have no reason to come looking for you.'

'You won't tell them?' said the Voice.

'If I was convinced you were no longer a threat, I wouldn't have any reason to,' I said.

'Very well,' said the Voice. 'No more observation. No contact of any kind. Now please leave this area as soon as possible. We find your presence . . . disturbing.'

The Voice stopped speaking, and I could feel whatever was behind it moving away, in a direction I could sense but not put a name to. In a few moments it was gone, leaving only Penny and me in the dark. I had to wonder just who or what I'd been negotiating with, and who or what it thought I was.

I couldn't help but smile. The conversations you get into that you never thought would happen . . .

A light appeared, up ahead. Sharp and fierce, as though someone had smashed a hole in the universe and let in the light from outside. The light at the end of the tunnel. It didn't grow any larger or brighter as I shot towards it, but it seemed to fill my eyes and my head to overflowing. And then I hit it, hard, and broke through to the other side.

I was standing on the open hillside, under a night sky full of stars and a reassuringly bright half-moon, with the hole behind me and Mike and the Professor before me, looking shocked and startled. They both started speaking at once, demanding to know where I'd been and what I'd been doing. I ignored them, and looked down at Penny in my arms. They quickly fell silent as they realized something was wrong.

'Is she dead?' said Mike, blunt as always.

'No,' I said.

'Is she all right?' asked the Professor.

'Yes,' I said. Because I needed that to be true.

Penny was breathing steadily, her eyes closed, her face calm and composed. She looked as she always did when she slept in my arms. I lowered her carefully to the ground, and checked her pulse. It seemed strong and regular. I didn't understand why she hadn't woken up, now we were out of the hole. The other Paul said he only shut her mind down to protect her from the strain of passing from one world to another. Or perhaps he simply didn't want her to see his world. My world. But I assumed she'd wake up the moment we were out of the hole and safely back on Earth. I was starting to worry the other Paul might have done something to her.

I leant over Penny till my face was almost touching hers, and said her name. Her eyelids fluttered, as though my breath had disturbed them, and then her eyes opened. She smiled slowly, happy that I was the first thing she saw. She started to sit up, and I helped her. Then I held her to me like I would never let her go, and she held me. And everything was all right again.

After a while we let go of each other and got to our feet. I was ready to help her, but she made it clear without saying anything that she didn't need any help. She's always been fussy about things like that. She brushed herself down, in that automatic way women have, and looked at the hole and then at me.

'All right! What the hell just happened?'

'You don't remember?' I said.

'No,' she said, frowning. 'I remember Paul grabbing me for no reason. And then running up the hill, carrying me. I fought him, but he was too strong . . . I remember you talking to Paul as we stood before the hole. And then it all went dark.'

'He took you with him into the hole,' I said. 'So I went in after you.'

'Of course you did,' said Penny. She smiled at me dazzlingly, and then hit me with a stern look. 'Of course I would have done the same for you . . .'

'Of course,' I said.

'You don't remember anything of what happened inside the hole?' the Professor said incredulously.

'No,' said Penny.

'Neither do I,' I said firmly. It seemed the safest way to go.

Mike made a loud frustrated noise. 'What a waste . . .'

I suddenly realized that my senses had returned to what they should have been all along. I could see all the way across the campsite, from one perimeter to the next, every detail sharp and clear. I could hear everyone's heartbeat, and the gentle rasp of their breathing. I could smell their individual scents, underneath their chosen perfumes. It felt like I'd been walking around wearing blinkers and earmuffs. Which had finally been torn away, letting the world back in. I couldn't believe I'd gone so long without being fully aware of the difference, without realizing the extent to which the hole had been messing with my head. I looked back at the hole, and saw immediately that it was smaller than it had been. The circle had shrunk from some seven feet in diameter to little more than five. The others saw the look on my face, followed my gaze, and made various sounds of shock and surprise.

'The hole is shrinking!' said the Professor. 'Collapsing in on itself . . . We're losing it!'

'This isn't going to end up like a black hole, is it?' said Penny. 'And drag the whole world in after it?'

'No,' I said. 'There's no increase in gravity. It's just . . . going away.'

'Just as you said it would, Professor,' said Mike.

The Professor had nothing to say to any of us. All her attention was fixed on the slowly disappearing hole.

'Does this mean we're finally free of the damned thing?' said Penny.

'Looks that way,' I said. I didn't add that it wouldn't be back. They'd only have wanted to know how I knew.

Penny sniffed loudly. 'Good riddance!'

'But now we'll never know what it was,' said the Professor. She stared at the gradually shrinking hole as though it was dying. 'One of the great mysteries of the world, disappearing in front of our eyes.'

'We know what it was,' Mike said flatly. 'It was a killing thing. We're better off without it.'

The Professor rounded on him, with such anger in her face that Mike actually fell back a step. The Professor's face was dangerously flushed, and her voice shook with open rage.

'This was our chance to open up a whole new field of knowledge! To make our names in the scientific community! To go down in history as the greatest pioneers of our age!'

'At least we're still alive,' said Mike.

'Yes, but . . .' said the Professor.

'You said the hole would disappear, Professor,' said Penny.

The Professor looked suddenly smaller, even defeated. 'I wasn't ready to let it go yet . . .'

'I'm not sure it would have done us any good to have had our names attached to the hole,' Mike said slowly. 'It was always going to be a poisoned chalice after what it did here.'

'It's all right for you,' said the Professor, not looking at him. 'You've still got a career. This was my last chance.'

I studied the hole carefully. I hoped the Voice had understood me and it would shut down all its spy holes. Unless . . . it was only responsible for this particular hole. In which case, who was watching us through the other holes? I'd have to talk to the Colonel about that, when I got back. I still wasn't sure exactly how much I'd be putting in my official report. I'd discovered a great many things in this mission that the Colonel didn't need to know. There was nothing in my agreement with the Organization that meant I had to give up my secrets, any more than the Organization had to be completely open with me.

And I had to wonder . . . If there were other holes, did that mean the other Paul could still come looking for me? Wearing another face, another body? He said he'd wait till Penny wasn't around any more, that he could afford to be patient. But I wasn't sure I believed him . . .

Penny tapped me lightly on the arm to get my attention, and when I looked round I found the Professor was glaring at me.

'What happened to Paul? Why didn't he come back with you?'

'I don't know,' I said. 'I remember going into the hole and coming out again. But that's it. I suppose he must still be in there.'

'So he won't be coming back?' said Mike.

'If he was going to come back,' I said, 'I think he would have done so by now . . . How long were Penny and I gone?'

'Just a few moments,' said Mike. 'We saw you dive in after them, but we'd only just got here when you and Penny came popping straight back out again. Almost like you'd been shot out by a catapult. Maybe the hole didn't want you and Penny, just Paul. Though why anyone would want him . . .' He looked at the hole with a surprisingly wistful expression. 'Maybe he went all the way through, to the other end of the tunnel. If Ellie's theory was right, he could be walking on some other world right now. I almost envy him. The things he must be seeing . . .'

'At least now we can be sure who the murderer was,' said the Professor.

We all looked at her.

'We can?' I said.

'Of course!' said the Professor. 'It has to be Paul! Why else would he attack Penny? Though why he took her into the hole . . . Perhaps because he was losing control of the situation. Everything that's happened here has been about control over the hole.'

'Go on,' I said.

'He must have realized the game was over when Mike said he was going to check up on everyone's background,' said the Professor.

Mike nodded quickly. 'Of course. I could have checked his face against the photo in his official file. That must have been what pushed him over the edge.'

'But why did he throw himself into the hole? And why did he want to take me with him?' said Penny.

'He needed a hostage, to keep us from taking him down,' said Mike. 'And anyway, he must have been out of his mind by that point, after everything he'd done. You saw how oddly he was behaving, at the end.'

'Odd, even for him,' said the Professor. 'But then he always was a bit too quiet for my liking.'

'He must have been a ringer,' Mike said wisely. 'A secret agent for some foreign power.'

'Well, possibly,' said Penny. 'But I still don't see why he chose to jump into the hole.'

'Once his cover was blown, his mission was over,' said Mike. 'He knew he couldn't get away, and he couldn't afford to be questioned and risk giving away who his superiors were.'

'But why take me with him?' said Penny.

'I don't know!' said the Professor. 'Maybe it was just spite and vindictiveness!' She looked at me impatiently. 'You're security, you must understand these people and how they think.'

'Sometimes . . .' I said. 'People can always surprise you. Let's go back to the fire. Sit down and get some rest. It's been a long night.'

'Right,' said the Professor. 'We can finally relax, now the murderer is gone. No more worrying and looking over our shoulder. Though I'm still not sure what I'm going to say to Mr Carroll when he calls.'

Mike checked his watch. 'It should be dawn soon. I'll be so glad to see the sun come up. I was beginning to think this night would go on for ever.'

We made our way back down the hill, and settled ourselves around the camp fire. Penny leaned companionably against my shoulder. The fire was on the brink of going out, so Mike fed it some more branches. The flames flared up, warm and comforting. Mike held his hands out to them. They weren't shaking any more. The Professor sat stiffly on her own, staring into the flames, intent on her own thoughts. I thought for a while too, turning things over in my mind and putting them together. Until finally I raised my voice to address everyone.

'It has been a long night,' I said, 'and a lot has happened in the dark. Many things are now clear to me, though I have a feeling some may never be properly explained. But I am now ready to say who the murderer really is.'

Penny sat up straight. Mike looked startled, and then shocked. The Professor just stared at me blankly.

'I thought we'd already decided the murderer had to be Paul?' said Mike, almost plaintively.

'No,' I said. 'The Professor's accusation was a good try, but it doesn't really hang together when you examine it closely. You accepted it because you wanted the killer to be gone, so you could relax. But the more I thought about it, the less the idea made sense. And if Paul wasn't the murderer, that meant the killer had to be sitting here at the fire. And once I thought that, it all fell into place. It was you, Professor Bellman. You killed Robert and Ellie, and possibly Terry.'

'What?' said Mike. He scrambled away from the Professor, putting as much distance as he could between the two of them. The Professor didn't move, didn't react, didn't say anything. Just stared unflinchingly back at me.

'Something you said just now gave me the final clue,' I said. 'Helped me to piece it all together. You said everything that happened here was about control over the hole. And who did the hole matter to most?

'As leader of this team you could be anywhere and never have to explain yourself. You could appear and disappear, because you had no distinct workstation to hold you in one place like the other scientists. And you were always on your own when someone was attacked. Everyone else had an alibi for at least one of the deaths. Apart from you, Professor.

'You were the one moving around in the dark, luring Penny and me to the part of the site furthest from the hole, so you could sneak back to it and attack Robert.

'You were the only one on your own when Ellie died. Paul was with Penny and me, Mike was in his tent. Also, you told me you'd looked into Ellie's tent and found she wasn't there, but when I looked I saw the tent flaps hadn't been opened. And when we heard the scream at the hole, that turned out to have been you. Not Ellie. You screamed after Ellie was dead, to confuse us as to the time of her death.

'To tie the deaths to the hole, you also made up that bit about the hole growing in size every time somebody died. All very clever, Professor, but all I had to do was put the clues together and they pointed straight to you.

'As the leader of the team, you could approach any of your people, for what would seem like perfectly good reasons, and get them to go wherever you wanted. None of them would feel in any danger, until it was too late. That's how you were able to persuade Ellie to go with you to the hole. You had the authority to order her to go. And like Robert before her, she didn't understand how dangerous it was to turn her back on you. Until you shoved her up against the side of the hole. You used the razor-sharp edge because you had no access to proper weapons, and because it enabled you to blame the deaths on the hole. But using the edge of the hole was a giveaway in itself: because that was a weapon that didn't need strength or skill, just cunning and determination.

'I think I'm ready to accept Terry's death as a well-intentioned accident, but you killed Robert and Ellie. I have to admit, I'm not really sure why. You said it was all about control of the hole. So that has to mean control of the research. Was that it? Did you just want all the glory for yourself?'

'I wouldn't expect you to understand,' said the Professor. Her voice and face were eerily calm. 'In the end, it's all about survival. Publish or perish has always been the driving force in the scientific community. You have no idea of the pressures involved. All those bright young minds they gave me for this project, basing their work on my theories . . . Typical of the vicious young predators always biting at my heels and looking for a chance to stab me in the back.

'I couldn't compete any more, I knew that. I was months away from being forced into retirement. Then the Colonel threw me this second chance. This wonderful mystery, with all kinds of grants and work on offer to those who could solve it . . . I was ready to work with the team, but they weren't interested in working with me. They ignored my advice, wouldn't let me help them, denied me this final chance to attach my name to a triumph. Their names, their theories, would be the only ones to go into the official report, and no one would ever know how much I contributed. I couldn't allow that.

'So, first rule of academia. Get them before they get you. You're right, of course, I had nothing to do with Terry's death. He took care of that all by himself, because he wouldn't listen to me. Though I have to wonder what he saw inside the hole that you didn't . . . Anyway, his death gave me the idea. If that appeared suspicious, why not use it to get rid of all the

people who were against me? The hole was such a mystery
it could be blamed for anything. And it did help that the locals
had this wonderfully vague legend about a Beast that I could
use to confuse things. This was my chance to seize the fame
and fortune that should always have been mine. I was damned
if I'd let them force me into retirement.'

'You killed my Ellie!'

Mike threw himself at the Professor, his outstretched hands
going for her throat. I grabbed him out of mid-air, slammed
him back into place, and then held him there until the fight
went out of him. The Professor didn't move, didn't even flinch.
When I finally let go of Mike, he just sat where he was, his
face twisted with grief.

'She killed my Ellie . . .'

'But you're not a killer,' I said. 'Don't let her make you
into one. The Professor will stand trial, and then be locked
away in a cage in some secret security establishment until she
rots. Her name and her work will be forgotten. That's punish-
ment enough for her.'

Penny looked disbelievingly at the Professor. 'You killed
Robert and Ellie, in that horrible fashion, just so you would
get the credit for the work here?'

The Professor smiled. A slow, quietly satisfied smile.

'The more deaths associated with the hole, the better. I was
going to kill all of you, one by one. You'd never have seen it
coming. Especially after I blamed it all on Paul. You'd never
have dreamed a dried-up old thing like me could be a threat.
And when I was the only one left, the poor traumatized survivor
of a terrible tragedy, I could tell any story I wanted . . .'

She stopped, and looked at me coldly. 'But you had to take
it all away from me. Well, to hell with them and to hell with
you! You're not putting me in prison . . . not while there's a
new world waiting.'

She jumped to her feet and ran up the hillside, heading for
the hole. We all got to our feet and ran after her. I could have
caught up with her easily, despite her head start, but I didn't.
The Professor reached the hole ahead of us. She didn't slow
down, didn't hesitate. Just jumped into the hole, and the darkness closed over her without a single ripple.

We all came to a halt before the hole, and it disappeared. As though one last sacrifice had been enough.

'She could come back,' Penny said finally. 'We did.'

'No,' I said. 'I don't think so.'

Penny shot me a look, hearing something in my voice that told her I knew more than I was telling, but she didn't say anything. Mike didn't notice the look. He was still staring at the brightly lit spot on the hillside where the hole used to be.

'Now we'll never know what it was,' he said finally. 'Still, there is an awful lot of recorded data. Enough for me to spend my whole life working on. And whatever papers I write, I'll make sure Ellie's name is always right there with mine.'

'She'd have done the same for you,' said Penny.

Mike smiled. 'Actually, she almost certainly wouldn't. Ellie was always very competitive.'

The smile disappeared as he kept looking at the hole. 'I suppose it's possible the Professor could end up wherever Paul went. Is it very wrong of me to hope it's the same awful place Terry saw?'

'No,' I said. 'Not wrong. Just human.'

'Ah well,' said Mike. 'Nobody's perfect.'

He turned his back on where the hole used to be and set off down the hill, heading back to the fire. Penny moved in beside me.

'At least you saved one, this time,' she said. 'Tell me, Ishmael . . . what did happen, inside the hole?'

'I'll tell you later,' I said. 'When we're alone.'

'Who's going to hear us out here, on the side of a hill?'

'You never know who might be listening,' I said, looking at where the hole used to be. I was already wondering how much it would be safe for her to know. Not for my protection, but for hers.

And then we both looked round sharply, as we heard Mike raise his voice in surprise. We raced back down the hill, to find Mike staring open-mouthed at Paul, who was sitting beside the fire looking very confused.

'Where did you go?' he said. 'I nodded off by the fire, and when I opened my eyes everyone had vanished.'

'You went into the hole!' said Mike. 'And took Penny with you!'

'I did?' said Paul, frowning. 'Why would I do something so stupid?' He looked at Penny. 'I'm really sorry . . . but I don't remember any of that.'

'There's a lot of not remembering going around,' said Penny. She shot me a hard look, making it clear she would expect an explanation later, and then shrugged. 'Maybe some things are just better forgotten.'

'I always miss out on the excitement,' said Paul. He looked at Mike. 'What happened while I was gone?'

'Well . . .' said Mike.

I led Penny away, leaving the two of them to talk. I was sure they had a lot to say to each other. I felt a little easier in myself. By returning the original Paul, his replacement had demonstrated a surprising amount of mercy. And that had to mean something. Maybe he was a better man than I'd thought.

And maybe I was too.